Last Stage from Hell's Mouth

Sam Cotton was the last person anyone in the town of Hope would have suspected of wrongdoing. All that changed, however, when Sam was caught riding hell-for-leather away from the scene of a robbery and murder. The townsfolk now see his future as being measured in hours, but Sam's father still believes in him – and only his father can save him.

Jim Cotton sets out on a desperate mission to prove his son's innocence, and every which way he turns brings increasing trouble. Outlaw gangs, old enemies, gun-fights, beatings, exhaustion and even the landscape conspire to keep him from saving Sam's life.

In this story of revenge, double-dealing, violence, and forbidden love, both Jim and Sam Cotton discover new depths of courage. Their whole future, and the future of Hope itself, will be changed forever.

Last Stage from Hell's Mouth

Derek Rutherford

A Black Horse Western

ROBERT HALE · LONDON

Typeset by
Derek Doyle & Associates, Shaw Heath
Printed and bound in Great Britain by
CPI Antony Rowe, Chippenham and Eastbourne

CHAPTER ONE

New Mexico Territory 1883

Jim Cotton's hammer crashed down on a red-hot length of iron and raised a shower of sparks. He lifted the hammer again just as someone put their hand on his back.

He turned around.

'Tessa,' he said, wiping a sleeve across his forehead. 'You surprised me.' He smiled, then noticed her expression. 'What's up?'

'You best come quickly, Jim.'

'What is it?'

'It's Samuel.'

Jim's heart quickened. 'What's happened?'

She shook her head. The absence of words scared him. 'Tessa?'

'There's about thirty of them – Jackson Kane's kin, Queenie Vega's boys, the Rodriguezes. More all the time.'

Despite the heat from his forge Jim Cotton felt a coldness sweep over him.

'What's this got to do with Samuel?'

That morning someone had robbed Irwin Foote's

mercantile. Jackson Kane, Queenie Vega, and Ima Rodriguez had all been caught in the crossfire when Irwin had pulled a gun on the robber. All three of them had died. Irwin took a bullet in the face. His jaw was smashed. He was still unconscious and no one expected him to live. It was the single worst thing to have happened in living memory in Hope, New Mexico, and that included anything that the Apache had ever done. All morning a fury had raged back and forth through the town like a terrible echo bouncing endlessly around a canyon. That someone could gun down two women and two old men for the sake of pennies demonstrated a depravity that few in Hope could conceive of. Even Jim Cotton, who had seen far worse more than twenty years before, but – thank God – not since, had felt that anger and disbelief. It was why he had gone back to work when so many other people were still standing on the street in a sense of shock. He had blown the coals to a white heat and had taken out his rage on a strip of red-hot metal.

He asked again. 'What's this got to do with Samuel, Tessa?'

Fear tightened Tessa's face. 'Some of those who were out looking for the killer saw a boy riding the west trail. When they went after him they say he took off like he had the Devil on his tail.'

Jim didn't need to ask the boy's name.

'No!' It was ridiculous. They all knew Samuel. They knew he was a good kid. They knew he wasn't a robber – let alone a killer.

'They just brought him in,' Tessa said. 'Old Montgomery said he saw the robber come out of the store. He said the boy they brought in was the same boy.'

Jim's arm started shaking. He strode across to his water barrel and plunged the tongs and the hot metal into the water. The iron sizzled and spat and steam rose up around him.

'Montgomery can't see past the end of his nose,' he said, hurrying to untie his leather apron, the simple knot was too intricate and tight for his suddenly weak and trembling fingers. He gave up and left the apron on.

'You better go quick, Jim,' Tessa said. 'They're fixing to hang him. They're fixing to hang him right now.'

Jim Cotton grabbed his Spencer rifle and ran. A crowd had formed outside the sheriff's office. Sheriff Benito Garcia was appealing for calm, desperately trying to make himself heard above the growing mob, but the crowd noise drowned the lawman out – people were yelling and swearing and spitting on the ground and laughing with terrible relief and calling for all manner of ungodly things to be done to the prisoner. Jim Cotton saw Garcia's deputy – Hector Lopez – standing alongside the sheriff on the raised walkway that fronted Garcia's office and jail. Both men cradled rifles and stood in front of the door. At one point someone started up the steps but Garcia stepped forwards and said something and the man paused, but when he tried to step back down into the street the crowd had pushed forward to fill the space that he had left. Women and children were joining the mass too, and way down the street in the distance Jim could see yet more people coming. There was even a dog on the opposite plank-walk, a lazy flea-ridden cur that never seemed to do anything but sleep, which had stood up to watch, its tail wagging

7

with interest at the excitement.

Several members of the mob spotted Jim. Someone reached out and grabbed his arm. Someone else said, 'Don't get involved, Jim. We're going to hang him and ain't nothing you can about it.' He brushed them aside and climbed the wooden steps to where the town's lawmen were standing.

The volume of abuse rose. A stone struck him on the shoulder. Someone started to follow him up the side steps and before he'd even had a chance to speak to the lawmen he found himself taking up station next to Garcia and Lopez, the three of them forming a triangle in front of the door, guns raised, determination etched on their faces.

'This is not the way!' Garcia yelled.

'He's a killer!' somebody shouted back. 'It's the *right* way!' A roar of agreement went up.

'We're going to hang him, Ben,' someone else called. 'Ain't nothing you can do to stop us either.'

The crowd pressed forwards.

'Nobody's hanging anyone,' Garcia shouted.

'You can't stop us! Not all of us. Not just two or three of you!' More cheers of approval erupted.

Garcia worked the action on his Winchester. 'He's my prisoner, no? You pay me good money to do my job and that's what I'm doing.'

'We pay your wages then you do as we say,' someone cried. 'And we say bring the prisoner back out.'

Jim Cotton noticed for the first time that a group of men at the front of the mob had a length of rope in their hands. On his left a couple of fellows were edging up on to the walkway.

'Laws is laws, people,' Garcia called. 'You did the right thing by bringing the kid in and giving him over into my custody. Now I do the right thing and keep him safe until he gets a fair trial.'

'He never gave my ma a fair trial!'

'Ain't that a fact! Bring him out!'

Jim heard the sound of Hector working the action on his rifle. The deputy looked at the men edging closer to Jim and said, 'You boys stop right there. I mean it.'

'It was a terrible thing this morning,' Garcia shouted. 'I'm not disputing it. And if the boy deserves to hang, then hang he will. But this is a good town and we're going to do this thing properly, yes?'

'We hear you, but we ain't listening,' someone said. 'Now step aside, Ben, or you're liable to get hurt, too.'

'Then you're going to have to hurt me,' the sheriff said.

'And me,' Hector said.

Jim couldn't speak. His throat was dry and his hands were shaking. He didn't believe the fear was for himself, but for Samuel, locked in a cage, he guessed, somewhere a few feet behind them.

'Judge Wilkes is due the day after tomorrow,' Garcia said, a little bit quieter now. Jim wondered if the man was lowering his voice on purpose, making the crowd quieten down in order to be able to hear what he was saying. 'We got the Casey boy to try for stealing horses from the McLean ranch and we got some legal matters around land disputes—'

'We don't want him added to a goddamn *list*,' someone – one of the Rodriguezes, Jim believed – yelled. 'We want him hanging from a roof.'

'Two days,' Garcia said. 'You give me two days.'

9

'*You* can have as many days as you want. The kid's got two minutes.'

The crowd squeezed forward again.

'This not the way!' Garcia yelled, his voice back to full volume.

'Killing three people ain't quite the same as a land dispute,' a women called out. Someone else said she was darn right, and with that one of the Rodriguez boys stepped up and tried to grab the sheriff's rifle. The sheriff yanked it backwards and as he did so the gun went off. Jim figured the bullet had gone harmlessly into the air but many in the mob didn't know that. So far as they were concerned the sheriff had just shot one of their own. They surged forwards. Someone pulled the rifle from Garcia's grasp, somebody else landed a haymaker on the side of the sheriff's head and his legs wobbled then gave way. Several men lifted Jim clean off the walkway and threw him down on to the street. The wind was knocked from him and for a moment he could neither see nor breathe. He did hear someone yelling for calm – Hector, he believed – but then another two shots were fired. A boot caught him in the temple and a heel ground against his teeth and the pain brought him up out of the fog. He tried to stand. Someone helped him, then he realized they weren't helping him up, they were restraining him, strong arms locking his own behind his back, a growl telling him to be easy, that there was nothing he could do now. He could taste blood in his mouth and he felt something trickling down his cheek. Blood, sweat, maybe tears. He squirmed, managed to stand, but couldn't free himself from the grasp of the man behind him. Years of hammering over the blacksmith's anvil had given him tremendous

10

strength in his arms, but the man had those arms twisted hard backwards and every movement sent shards of pain into Jim's shoulders and neck.

'Easy, Jim,' the man said again.

It was impossible to see the door to the jail. There was a mass of townsfolk pushing to get in. Then someone yelled that they had the bastard and to make some room.

Jim gritted his teeth and renewed his struggling. That was his son. His only son. He had no idea where his Spencer had gone. He had no recollection of dropping it, but it wasn't in his hands. No matter, he thought. He twisted and turned and tried to stamp backwards on his restrainer's foot. Pain sliced from his shoulders to the crown of his head. He screamed, not out of fear but to give himself strength, and he felt his arms pulling from the man's grip.

'Don't do this, Jim,' the man said.

There was the sound of revolver hammer being ratcheted back.

'Just hold still, Mr Cotton,' a second man said, and Jim felt the barrel of the gun being pressed against his neck. A redness came down over one eye, a blurring over the other. The crowd was shrieking and screaming like Indians racing in for a kill. All around him people were jostling and pushing to get closer to something he couldn't see. He recognized no one, all his friends, customers, and suppliers, had become deadly and evil strangers.

He tried to see who was holding the gun against him but it hurt too much to turn his head. Through the crowd he thought he saw a man with a rope high up on the second storey of the sheriff's building. There was a balcony up there and when he tried to blink the blood and

11

tears from his eyes he saw an image burned on to his retina of the man throwing a rope down off this balcony.

'Here's the sonofabitch!' someone yelled, and though Jim couldn't see Samuel he did see a hand reach up and grab the noose and pull it down.

'Ain't your fault the boy went bad,' the man behind him said. 'Blame the girl.'

The rope was pulled tight and suddenly he could see Samuel, the noose around his neck, his head being pulled upwards, blood all over his face, his skin ghost white where it wasn't bleeding, terror in his eyes.

'No!' Jim cried. 'Please!'

The fellow on the balcony was easing the rope around a thick wooden baluster as unseen hands below continued to pull it. He could see Samuel's head tilting to one side, knowing his son must be on the very tips of his toes now.

He opened his mouth to beg one more time but instead of his own voice he heard someone else cry, 'Stop! This is not the way! Stop right now!'

For a moment nothing happened. The fellow on the balcony worked another couple of inches of rope around the baluster and Samuel's head tilted even further to one side, the crowd still roared in anger and laughed in awful relief, and the man behind him still held Jim Cotton's arms tight. But almost imperceptibly everything paused. There was a change in the mob. Jim saw people's attention flit briefly from Samuel over to an old man and an old lady who were pushing their way through the crowd. Suddenly folk weren't sure where the centre of attention was.

'Get out the way, old lady,' someone shouted, but almost immediately someone else told the heckler to shush, that it

12

was Jackson Kane's widow there. Now Jim recognized the old man, too. Raoul Vega. Queenie's husband. The two of them had both lost their spouses in that morning's killing. Raoul even had a six gun in his hand although the old man was holding it down by his thigh as if he wasn't quite sure what to do with the weapon.

'This is not the way,' Raoul said.

'You know this isn't the way,' Martha Kane repeated. 'You know this isn't the *right* way.' She paused, and added quietly, '*Our* way.'

The crowd was stilled by the old couple. Jim figured that it was one thing being told to stop by a lawman, but it was another thing if those telling you to stop were the ones that had suffered the greatest loss.

'We didn't fight the Mexicans and the Rebs and we ain't fighting the Indians just to become savages ourselves,' Raoul said. 'You kill the boy this way and you're as bad as he is. This ain't the frontier lands where justice has to be served in whatever manner possible. We've built ourselves a respectable town here. We have laws.' He paused. 'Tomorrow I bury my wife and my friends. Let us think of them not . . . him. The day after, they tell me, the judge is in town.' He paused again and glanced around the crowd, then he looked over at Samuel. The rope must have loosened a little for Sam's head was back at its normal angle, although the terror in his eyes was anything but normal. 'But if the judge declares this boy guilty then I'll rope him up myself.'

That raised an uneasy laugh from some, a murmur of agreement from others. Jim felt the man behind him loosening his arm-lock.

'Now get on back to where you should be,' Martha Kane cried. 'Please let Raoul and me and Julio Rodriguez mourn in peace. Don't do anything shameful. Please respect us.' She paused, then added. 'Respect yourselves.'

Jim bowed his head. His arms were released but he didn't have the emotional or physical strength to turn and see who had been holding him. For a few seconds everyone stood still, confused, deflated. Then the fellow up on the balcony started pulling the loose end of the rope back up from those who had released it below.

'I ain't untying this noose,' he said. 'I respect what Mrs Kane and Mr Vega said, but my money's on us needing this rope day after tomorrow anyway.'

Slowly, the crowd broke up, small groups of men and women drifted away, all discussing what had just happened. Jim sank to his knees in the middle of the road. Out of the corner of his eye he spied the dog on the opposite plank-walk turn a few lazy circles, lie down, and appear to go to sleep immediately. Jim's heart was still pounding, his shoulders still hurt, his face ached and his mind was numb. Twenty feet away he saw Benito Garcia struggle to a standing position using his rifle as a lever to help himself up. The man's face was bloodied and his shirt was torn. Samuel was on his knees just outside the sheriff's door. Someone had taken the rope from around his neck but his hands were tied behind his back, his head was bowed. Next to Garcia, Hector Lopez was also struggling to stand.

Jim got to his feet.

'Sam,' he said, and realized he had no idea what to say next. He stumbled towards his son. 'Sam,' he said again.

Samuel looked up. 'Pa,' he said, and started to cry.

14

CHAPTER TWO

Sheriff Benito Garcia took the pot off the stove in the corner of his office and poured out four coffees. He opened a drawer in his desk and pulled out a bottle. Without asking he poured a shot of whiskey into each of the cups and then placed them in front of the men.

'*Gracias*,' Hector Lopez said. He was smoking a cigarette and stretching his neck one way then the other. One of his eyes was swollen and when the men had first come inside the sheriff's office after the crowd had dispersed, Jim had watched Hector twist the little finger of his left hand back into its socket. 'Someone trod on me,' Hector had said, as the dislocated finger snapped back in. 'They didn't mean it.'

Sheriff Garcia slumped behind his desk, sighed heavily, and took a sip of the steaming whiskey-laden coffee.

Samuel Cotton sat to one side. There was blood, dirt and tear tracks on his face and rope welts around his neck. But the biggest wound was in his eyes. They held nothing but emptiness now. The realization of what one man, or many, could do to another came to everyone sooner or later. Jim Cotton had first seen it at Glorieta Pass, when, as a volunteer, he'd been part of Major John Chivington's army. Other folks got to see what their fellow human beings were capable of when they came across farms that the Indians had come across first. But it was one thing seeing such things in war or at the hands of the Apache, it was another when it was your friends and neighbours doing it and when it was you that they were doing it to.

'How are you feeling, Sam?' Garcia asked.

Sam held the coffee cup in trembling hands. It looked to Jim as if he was freezing cold, but outside the August sun was blazing down with a ferocity that could burn a man's skin as sure as any forge could.

'I'm OK,' Samuel said.

'You want a cigarette?' Hector Lopez asked.

'No. I mean, yes. Thank you.'

'I'll roll it for you,' Hector said, looking at Sam's hands.

'You're the luckiest fellow in the territory this afternoon, I reckon,' Garcia said. 'No?'

'I didn't do anything,' Sam said, and his hands convulsed so much that he spilt coffee over his ripped trousers.

'Seems like just about everyone in town thinks otherwise,' Garcia said.

'He didn't do anything,' Jim said, aware of his own hands shaking and his voice trembling. His mouth and eyes felt full of grit and a ringing echoed in his ears. His own voice felt distant, as if it was coming from someone else. 'If he said he didn't do anything, then he didn't.'

'You were lucky the ones who found you did.' Hector Lopez said. 'Many of the others would have hanged you there and then.'

'I was just riding around. I didn't even know there'd been a shooting.'

'Couple of the townsfolk said they saw you clear as day,' Garcia said.

'I wasn't even in town.'

'Where were you?'

'Just riding around.'

'Up on the west trail?'

'Yes.'

'Just riding around? High noon in August, yes? And then you took off running when they came after you. Why do that if you had nothing to hide?'

'I . . . I didn't know who it was.'

'Sam,' Jim said, 'what were you doing out there? If there's something you need to tell us, then tell us. I know you didn't shoot anyone in town. I think Benito and Hector know that too. But, like they say, no one rides around up there on day like today for no reason.'

Hector Lopez stood up and passed the made cigarette to Samuel. Hector flicked a Lucifer into life with his thumbnail and Samuel breathed smoke deep into his lungs. He grimaced and coughed.

'Hurts?' Hector Lopez asked.

'Yes. Thank you.'

'Pleasure.'

'You finish your cigarette and coffee, Sam,' Garcia said. 'And I'm going to have to lock you up again.'

'I didn't do anything!'

'Day after tomorrow Judge Wilkes is due in town. He's the one you got to persuade, not me. But let me tell you,

Sam, you're going to need a good story. A better story than you've got so far. There's a lot of folks out there swear that it was you.'

'Sam,' Jim said, 'what made you ride away when you saw those folks coming after you?'

'I . . . I don't know.'

Hector Lopez pressed out the stub of his cigarette on the sheriff's desk and then took a long pull of coffee. 'Judge Wilkes going to be impressed with that.'

'Sam,' Jim said again, but again was at a loss to know what to say. He felt powerless, and he felt ashamed because of that powerlessness. Out there he should have done more. This was his son, his only kin. And it had taken two old folks to stop the lynching.

'Pa?' Samuel said.

'I . . . I ain't gonna let them hang you, son. Don't you worry.'

'If Wilkes finds your boy guilty you ain't gonna have a choice,' Hector Lopez said.

'I'm not guilty!'

'So you keep saying.'

'Listen,' Garcia said, 'I have to lock you up again, now. For your own safety as much as anything. I'm sorry I wasn't able to do better for you out there. I don't feel good about that.'

'You did your best,' Sam said. 'Thank you.'

'That's what y'all pay me for,' Garcia said. 'Now come on out back again. You know the way, yes?'

Nobody would meet Jim's gaze as he wandered back towards his blacksmith shop. He saw one of the Rodriguez

18

boys spit on the ground as he passed, but he couldn't be sure that the boy wasn't just spitting anyway.

It seemed to Jim that the town of Hope had now lost the very thing that the early settlers had named it for. It felt as dry and as empty as the skeletons of dead horses and cattle out there in the desert, their rib-cages picked clean and gleaming white in the sun, all life long gone. These people had been their friends. Samuel had grown up with them. They knew him. How could they do this? How could they *believe* this?

'Jim. Jim, are you all right?' It was Tessa Brown again, hurrying to catch up with him. 'How's Samuel? I saw. . . . It was dreadful.'

She was a pretty woman, dark hair, big eyes, not too skinny but not too plump either. Jim had known her over ten years. She'd taken over as the schoolmarm after his wife Mary-Anne died at only twenty-eight years old. It had been the hardest time in Jim's life. His father had died just six months before Mary-Anne. One day they had been a big happy family, three generations, and six months later there was just Jim and Samuel.

'Dreadful doesn't come close, Tess,' Jim said, not slowing. 'How could they do that?' He looked across at her as they walked, anger in his eyes and his voice.

'I don't know,' she said, slightly out of breath.

He slowed. 'And there was damn all I could do about it!' He held up the Spencer. It had been left in the street after the crowd had cleared. 'They took this off me. They held me back. How do you think I feel? I couldn't even protect my own.'

'It's not your fault, Jim.'

There were lengthening shadows on their side of the street now. Jim shivered. 'I couldn't even protect my boy.'

'I understand, but—'

'No you don't. How could you?'

'Why not? Because I have no children of my own?'

They were outside his shop now. He paused. 'Look, Tess, I'm sorry. All these people . . . they've known Sam since all he could do was crawl along the plank-walk. They *know* he didn't do this. Another few seconds and he'd have been. . . . I can't even begin to understand. That mob. The whole lot of them. My *friends*, Tess. Or at least people that used to be. They won't even look at me now. It's like something has taken them over. How can I forgive them? And that's nothing compared to how I feel about myself. I let them do it—'

'No you didn't! You tried—'

'*I let them do it*, Tess. Sam is everything to me. They should've had to kill me first and in the end it was Raoul Vega and Martha Kane who did what I wasn't able to do.'

She reached out a hand but he turned away, tears burning his eyes, acid burning his throat.

'How can I forgive myself?' he said.

He didn't invite her in, but he didn't stop her when she followed him and stoked the stove and filled a pan with water and coffee beans. He rolled a cigarette and stood with his back to Tessa, looking out of the window over main street. He watched the people out there talking and now and again glancing over at the blacksmith's shop. He watched their shadows writhe on the floor like something evil. And that was the truth of it. There was evil in these people. Where it had come from he didn't know. Maybe it was there all along and it just took the murderous bullets from someone's gun to free it.

'Coffee,' she said. 'Have you got anything strong to go in it?'

'You sound like the sheriff.'

'Sorry?'

'Coffee and liquor seems to be the standard fare around these parts for getting over the lynching of a son.'

'I didn't mean—'

'It's OK. It was a bad attempt at . . . I don't know.' He took a long pull on his cigarette, wondered briefly what she was doing here, laughed once at himself without knowing why or feeling the least bit amused about anything, and said, 'In the white cupboard. Cheapest whiskey in the territory. Best go easy with it.'

She laced both drinks, handed one to him, and sat down on an old wooden chair by his table.

'So,' she said, 'how is Sam?'

He drank some of the coffee. The heat and the rotgut whiskey burned his throat. For a moment he wondered if she was being clever, using her schoolmarm training to take his mind off himself and on to something else. Then he realized that thinking of something – some*one* – else was exactly what he ought to be doing and that his self-centredness was both selfish and wrong. And that thought made him wonder if Tessa was actually reprimanding him in a very subtle and underhand way. Then the cheap liquor reached his belly and he realized he was thinking too hard and too much and all she was doing was asking after Sam.

21

'He's scared,' Jim said.

'I think anyone would be.'

'He can't believe they'd do this to him. Just like I can't believe it. He says he was just up on the west trail riding around. But he won't say what he was doing up there. Both Garcia and Lopez say he's going to need a better story for the day after tomorrow when Judge Wilkes is due in town.'

'And he won't say? Not even to save his life?'

'Not even to save his life.'

Later, when Tessa had gone back to her schoolhouse lodgings, and night had fallen over Hope, Jim Cotton took a large pitcher out to the town well. He had just lowered the bucket when he sensed someone approaching him from behind. He turned, sensing trouble in a town where he'd never had trouble before. It was a woman. She stood motionless maybe ten yards back, and never said a word. He couldn't make out who it was, the moon was bright behind her.

'Evening, ma'am,' he said.

She never replied.

Jim turned back to the deep well and hoisted up the bucket. He poured as much water as he needed into his pitcher, and then turned to go.

The woman said, 'I know you think he didn't do it. That he couldn't do it. But your boy's been seeing a rich girl. And the word is he simply never had enough money to hold on to her.'

'What do you mean, a rich girl?' A throwaway comment from earlier in the day came back to him: *Ain't your fault the boy went bad. Blame the girl.*

'None so blind as those that don't see,' the woman said.

Jim reached out to grab her, water spilling from his jug.

'Don't touch me,' she hissed. 'I can see where the boy got his short fuse from.'

'What rich girl?' he said, letting go of her arm.

'The McLean girl,' she said. 'She's very pretty but she's not worth dying over.'

CHAPTER THREE

Deputy Hector Lopez was asleep when Jim Cotton opened the sheriff's office door. Hector's feet were up on Garcia's table, his hat pulled down over his eyes, and a rifle was laid across his lap. There was a cup on the table by his feet, and alongside it a small leather pouch that, Jim guessed, contained Hector's makings.

Jim closed the door gently.

When he looked back Hector was wide awake, the rifle levelled at Jim's stomach.

'Visiting hours finished long ago,' he said.

'I need to see him.'

Hector pondered on this for a moment, then said, 'He's locked up for his own good as much as anyone else's.' He swung his legs off the table. 'Don't try anything cute. I've never lost a prisoner before.'

'I'm not here to break him out,' Jim said, although if he were honest there had been a fleeting moment when he had opened that door and seen the deputy asleep that the idea had flashed across his mind. A second later the more frightening thought had followed that if all that lay between his son and the townsfolk was a sleeping deputy then it would be easy for *anyone* to break him out.

'You got ten minutes.'

There were three cages in the Hope jail in a room at the back of the office. One cage was empty. In another, Floyd Casey, the alleged horse thief, lay curled on a mattress, snoring. In the third cage Samuel sat with his back to the wall, arms wrapped around his knees, eyes staring through the bars at the door.

'Sam,' Jim said.

'Pa. What is it?'

'I heard something. Out on the street.'

Sam's eyes flicked from his father to Hector who was standing in the doorway, arms folded but still cradling the rifle.

'I'll wait outside,' Hector said, 'if you want to talk in private. But I'm not moving Floyd.' He walked back into the outer office and closed the door.

'What did you hear, Pa?' Sam said. He hadn't moved. He still sat in the far corner of the cell, looking smaller and younger than he was.

'Someone told me you've been seeing Amelia McLean.'

There was a long silence, broken only by Floyd Casey's long vibrant snores. Eventually Sam took his arms from his knees and stood up. Jim heard the sound of a joint popping in one of Sam's knees or elbows. His son walked over to the bars, wrapped his fists around them. Jim noticed the skin around Sam's wrists was raw.

'So what, Pa? So what if I have?'

'Is that why you were out there on the west trail? You were either coming or going from McLean's place?'

'She's a sweet girl, Pa. There's nothing wrong with us seeing each other.'

'Then why are you so scared of anyone finding out?'

Sam looked down at the floor. He swallowed and then breathed out heavily. When he looked back up Jim saw that there was a sheen of tears in his eyes. 'I don't know what's happened between you and Mr McLean, Pa, but he told Amelia that if ever he suspected she was seeing me then he'd whip the hide off her legs and marry her off to a fellow of his choosing even before the blood had stopped running.'

Now it was Jim's turn to look away, his own emotions raging.

'We were gonna run away, Pa,' Sam said. 'Soon, too.'

'And you're prepared to hang for her?'

'Would you've hanged for Ma?'

'That's different.'

'Why is it different?'

'I don't know. It just is. Your ma and I were married. We—'

'You wouldn't have hanged for her before you were married?'

'This is a stupid conversation, Sam. I'm not going to let you hang when there's someone out there who can say exactly where you were.'

'I don't want Mr McLean hurting her. If he finds out about us. . . . She told me she'd seen him whip people before. He'll do it.'

'The townsfolk already know about you two. What makes you think he doesn't?'

'If he knew already he'd have stopped Amelia seeing me.'

26

'You're really prepared to let them hang you? What about me? Have you thought about me?'

'Pa, they ain't going to hang me. No judge is going to hang me when I never did nothing. Not these days.'

'You're right there. No one is going to hang you.'

'You ain't going to see him, are you, Pa?'

'Damn right I am.'

'Pa!'

'First thing in the morning.'

'He'll whip her! He'll take her away!'

'I'm going to save your life, Sam. Nothing else matters.'

CHAPTER FOUR

That night sleep came hard to Jim Cotton. Initially he rose every few minutes from his cot and peered out of the window and along main street, watching for a mob that he was sure would come. But there was no one out there. The sound of stealthy footsteps and muffled whispers that he believed he could hear was nothing more than the desert wind rustling through town. Later, as his eyes become sore with tiredness, he fell into short periods of sleep and dreamed vividly of the man on the balcony, the image as clear in his sleep as it had been against the insides of his eyelids earlier.

The next morning, before sunup, Jim Cotton drank a scalding cup of coffee, smoked a cigarette, then fed and saddled Molly, his mule. Even if he pushed her hard it was a couple of hours' ride out to Skunk McLean's ranch, and the coolness of the early morning would make it easier on both of them.

That, and the fact that Jim wanted to get this situation sorted out as soon as possible.

Jim's father, Joshua, and McLean's pa Charles, had

headed west into New Mexico territory together back in '51. They'd been part of a wagon train all the way from Tennessee. The call had gone out for teachers and preachers and doctors and builders, seamstresses and smiths, stonemasons and woodsmen and metalworkers and everyone else under the sun. But mostly it was the call of gold and of limitless opportunity that the men heard. There was talk of Indians, of course, but back then – even though the Mexican war was over – it was the Mexicans of whom most people were afraid. Jim and Skunk had been ten years old on that wagon train. Every day had been an adventure. It was a friendship that both boys thought would last forever.

But Charles McLean had found a seam of silver and Joshua Cotton hadn't, and although Jim had always understood the two men had been partners it turned out that money could make a man forgetful of such agreements.

So the families' fortunes and paths digressed, Joshua Cotton set up as a blacksmith, in a town that at the time was little more than tents and dust, and which everyone who settled there came to know as Hope. Charles – and his son Skunk – worked their claim and slowly became ever richer, eventually moving out of Hope to build a fortressed horse ranch in the shadows of the Santa Rita mountains where his mine lay, and from where he sent weekly teams of mules to the stamping mills and furnaces at Hell's Mouth.

In '62, Jim, now twenty-one years old, volunteered for Major John Chivington's Union Army. Skunk never joined up, instead staying at home and working the silver vein with his father and a growing team of employees. Skunk always accused Jim of looking down upon him because of his choosing not to fight, but Jim assured him that wasn't the case, that he'd joined up for adventure and nothing more. But it was yet another division between the two families. Jim fought at Valverde and Glorieta Pass. He learned how to shoot well and he learned how to kill. He learned how to drive a team of horses, too, and when the war was over – it didn't last long in New Mexico Territory – he took a job driving a stagecoach on the long and tough Hope to Hell's Mouth line. Charles McLean, suffering too many robberies and raids against his silver ore mule trains, had offered Jim twice the money that the stagecoach company paid, saying a man who could lead horses and kill men deserved proper pay. But Jim had politely refused. Already the families had grown far enough apart that honour was more important than money.

It was through his job driving the stagecoach that Jim met the beautiful Laurie St Louis. She was the daughter of the stagecoach line's division manager and now that Hope was prospering, with some of the houses and business made of brick – most of which were brought back from Hell's Mouth by McLean's returning mule trains – the St Louis family were talking of settling there. Hell's Mouth – not its real name, but the name by which everyone knew it now the stamping mills and furnaces and kilns were burning and pounding night and day – was rapidly becoming less attractive. The frontier had moved further west and Hope's roots were growing deeper and more permanent. Jim and Laurie spent days together in Hell's Mouth when his timetable allowed and he decided that once she'd moved to Hope he would ask her to marry him.

Except Skunk got there first.

And for all the broken promises around their fathers' prospecting, for all the perceived jealousy around riches or believed cowardice over the war, or the snub of turning down a well-paid job because of who was offering it, Jim knew that the straw that finally broke the back of any possible reconciliation between the two families was the stealing of Laurie St Louis.

Blame the girl, the words came back to him now.

Maybe it had been money, the promise of money, or maybe a vivid description of a life filled with no money, Jim never found out. All he knew was that one time, when he came home from the Hell's Mouth run he heard the news that Laurie was now with McLean.

He'd actually ridden up to the McLean ranch that day, still tired and dirty from the stage run. He'd taken a gun, fully intending to use it on his love rival – or so he'd thought. But, as it happened, he'd maintained his temper and his dignity and walked away with only his pride hurt.

In the long run the loss of Laurie St Louis worked in his favour. She'd been his first woman and maybe that clouded his judgement. Oh, he'd loved her, he'd loved her deeply. But later, when he met Mary-Anne Slade, a passenger on his coach, he fell even further in love. They married, and shortly afterwards, in '64, along came Samuel.

Now he was retracing that old ride up to McLean's stronghold, and again, it was because of a woman.

The sun was hot on his bare forearms and the back of his neck as he rode over the last rise and saw the ranch spread below him. It had been a long time since he had been out here and the expansion of the property shocked him. The house itself, built of brick and stone, was bigger than even the hotel back in Hope. The corrals and bunk houses surrounding it had grown, too. There was a lake over on the far side of the house where it looked like McLean had diverted and dammed one of the creeks that flowed out of the mountains. There was even a rowing boat on the lake and a boathouse with a wooden platform out front. Everything was surrounded by walls, fences, and wire.

Jim noticed several men with rifles standing at key points around the perimeter. The threat of attack from the Apaches was ever present, if, these days, rare, and out here away from the security of the town one had to be extra careful. That said, the word was that McLean had struck some kind of deal with the Indians and they left him alone. Jim didn't know if that was true or not, but he did know that he'd been spotted. One of the guards down there had called across to another man and the two of them were talking and pointing up at him.

He rode down towards the wide gate above which swung a very ornate metal sign that read McLean's Double M. Although McLean did dabble in some ranching most folks understood the Double M to stand for McLean Mining.

The gate swung open as he approached. Skunk McLean himself was standing on the far side. He was a big man, wide across the chest, belly, and face. His hair was curly and grey and flowed out from beneath a brown hat. His face was weathered and lined like old leather. He wore a brown corduroy suit and polished boots. He had a china cup and saucer in one hand, a cigar in the other. Slid into his right boot was a riding crop. It was his weapon of choice. Not deadly, but it could leave a permanent scar when whipped across a man – or woman's – face.

'Jim Cotton,' McLean said. 'To what do we owe the pleasure?'

Behind him Jim heard the gate close. He was aware of several of McLean's hands standing around the yard.

'There's no pleasure in my visit.'

'Then I shan't offer you a cup of tea.' McLean raised the china cup, the cigar held firmly between two fingers, and gently sipped his drink.

'I've come to see Amelia.'

McLean stared up at him for long seconds. He took another sip of his tea. 'She's rather young for you, Cotton.'

'Funny.'

McLean said, 'I heard there was some trouble in town yesterday.'

Jim Cotton felt his neck burning. Dust swirled around McLean's polished boots. Steam from the china cup framed his face.

'Nothing a bit of truth won't put right.'

'Truth, eh?'

'You know Sam wouldn't hurt anyone.'

McLean took a long pull on his cigar. He tilted his head up and to the right and blew the smoke from his lungs.

'How's the iron business? You know, we should talk sometime. I might be able to put some work your way. Lots of work for a smith here.'

Through McLean's cigar smoke Jim saw movement. Over in the big house, standing in the doorway, he could see Laurie McLean. She was too far away for him to be able to see her expression. But there was something about the way she stood, the tenseness in her body, the angle of her head, that made him think she was nervous. Or perhaps it was just his imagination.

He looked back at McLean. 'Business is fine.'

'Good. Business problems *and* family problems would be a little too much to bear, wouldn't it?'

'Amelia,' he said. 'Can I talk to her, please? It'll only take a moment.'

'How on earth do you figure that talking to my daughter is going to help you?'

'You know how.'

'Indulge me.'

'She was with Sam yesterday morning.'

McLean shook his head. 'I don't think so.'

'Let her tell me that.'

'Like I said, I don't think so.'

'You'd let Sam hang just because he's a Cotton? Just because of . . . old times?' He resisted looking over at Laurie again.

'Don't flatter yourself, Jim. I've got nothing against you or your boy. Look at all of this.' He swung his cigar-holding hand in a wide arc, vaguely indicating the house and the other buildings, the corrals and the horses, the cowboys, the lake, even the mountain. Especially the mountain, Jim thought. It was the mountain that made McLean every penny he owned. The rest was just him playing at being a rancher. 'You think I care about you or your boy?'

'I'm hoping you care about justice.'

'I don't have the time or indeed the inclination to worry about every crime and every punishment.'

'This isn't every crime, Skunk. This is my son and your daughter's—'

'It's nothing to do with Amelia.' McLean's words came too fast and were too hard.

'You're lying.'

'There's nothing for you here, Cotton. I'm sorry, but you've had a wasted ride.'

'Let me see her, Skunk. Let Amelia make up her own mind.'

McLean looked over Jim Cotton's shoulder. 'Open the gate, Mitchell. Mr Cotton is leaving.'

Molly wasn't fast. Especially not after a long hot trek like she'd had that morning. But when Jim Cotton flicked her with his heels and urged her forwards, not towards the gate, but to the woman standing over in the doorway of the main house, she'd made twenty yards before McLean or any of his men realized what was happening.

'Go, girl!' Jim urged, as they rushed alongside the cut-pine fence of a corral and kicked up dust as they turned towards the house.

He saw Laurie standing straighter, surprise in her body language, and behind him he heard the snap of a rifle action being worked. His back tingled and his buttocks tightened. A bullet now wouldn't help Sam one little bit. But it was too late. He'd made his call.

'Don't shoot,' McLean yelled behind him, and Jim thought that old friendships and long miles travelled together might count for something after all. A moment later, as he pulled Molly up just a few yards in front of

Laurie, he realized that McLean simply didn't want any of his men shooting towards his house, towards his wife.

'Laurie,' Jim said, a little breathlessly, resisting the urge to look behind him to see how close McLean and his boys were, and trying not to think about what was going to happen when they caught up with him.

Laurie McLean, once Laurie St Louis, back in the day when both their futures could have been so different, opened her mouth to say something. But Jim carried on talking, the words coming out fast.

'I need to speak to Amelia. You know she and Sam have been. . . . She was with him yesterday when someone robbed the mercantile. They say it was Sam but he was with Amelia and if she'll tell—'

'She's gone, Jim.'

Her words were quiet, resigned. Her eyes told him that she didn't agree with the decision, that she hadn't even been consulted. Her face told him the story, too. The once beautiful face, the *still* beautiful face, but one that had faced endless days of dry heat and sand and grit carried on the hot wind, the pain of bearing and nurturing a child, the constant battle and worry of surviving out here on the edge, and maybe, Jim thought with a sense of bitterness, of simply being with McLean, had taken the glow from her skin and the shine from her eyes and hair.

Her words hung in the air between them, sucking the oxygen from his own lungs, rendering him speechless.

'He sent her away,' Laurie said. She looked up at the sky. Later he wondered if she had been offering a prayer, maybe asking the heavens to look after Amelia, or maybe asking for forgiveness for not fighting to keep her at home. Or perhaps she was asking for her own escape. But right then he figured she was just looking at the sun and working out how many hours her daughter had been gone.

'He sent her down to Station Five this morning at first light.'

Her lips started to tremble. Her eyes glistened and then tears started to fall. She tried to hold it together, but then Jim Cotton heard heavy breathing behind him, felt someone grabbing his shoulder and pulling him backwards off Molly and, as he fell he saw Laurie's face crumple, heard her say, 'I'm sorry, Jim', then she was turning back into the cool darkness of her house whilst he was thrown to the ground. Someone kicked him hard in the back, and another boot connected with his head. He curled as tightly as possible and although the kicks continued for a few seconds he soon heard McLean say 'Stop, stop. Stop, boys.'

Then, 'Get up, Cotton.'

He unfolded himself. A vision of the lynch mob kicking and trampling him the day before flitted across his mind. He was getting too old to take such punishment. There was dirt and grit in his mouth again. He could taste blood. It felt like several knives had pierced his back. But he refused to let McLean see any pain in his expression.

'Now get out,' McLean said.

McLean stood to one side. His men did the same. There was a clear route back to the gate.

'You sent her away,' Jim Cotton said, shaking his head.

'I don't owe you any explanations.'

The riding crop was in McLean's hand now. McLean's

wrist twitched and the whip buzzed in the air. Jim Cotton figured McLean didn't even know he was doing it.

'You've got everything, but you've got nothing,' Jim said, picturing again the fear and regret in Laurie's eyes. The gleam and laughter that was now missing from those eyes.

The riding cropped whistled in the air again. He knows that I've seen the change in Laurie, Jim Cotton thought.

'She was going East anyway,' McLean said.

'Hell of a coincidence.'

'Amelia can have anything she wants. Back East the whole world can be hers.'

'You threatened to whip her and marry her off if she kept seeing Sam.' Jim Cotton spat blood on to the dry ground.

The whip whistled and cracked against McLean's own boot.

'Time to go, Cotton. I hope it works out for Sam.'

'This isn't finished.'

'Oh, I think it is.' Now he slipped the riding crop back into his boot. 'Give me that.' McLean took a rifle from one of his men, worked the action, and pointed it at Cotton. 'Like I said, time to go.'

Jim Cotton stared at the man who, as a boy, had travelled west with him. Together they had played alongside the trundling wagons, caught rabbits and fish, sang songs, made up stories, and wondered in amazement at the rivers and the plains and the mountains they first saw across vast distances, then slowly approached, and finally passed. Until here, on the very edge of the territories, they'd all settled in a town called Hope.

Jim touched Molly lightly on the rump, she turned, and together he and she walked slowly towards the gate, that tingling feeling in the centre of his back – where a bullet would hit – now stronger than ever.

In the army it felt like all they ever did was walk. Walk here, walk there. Walk to get water, walk back. Walk to get wood for the fires. Walk for three days, nerves as tight as violin strings, to a battle that never happened and walk three days back. Walk for a week just to be somewhere so that there *wouldn't* be a battle. Eventually walking to a battle that really happened, the nerves now shredded and the relief of actually doing something almost better than walking – until the fighting and the screaming and the dying actually began.

But such agonies aside, all they did was walk, and when it was over, Jim Cotton swore he would spend as little time walking in future as possible. So he got himself a job running a team of horses. It was a skill he'd picked up in Chivington's army, hauling cannons here and there whenever he could get himself assigned to such non-walking details. The Territory Stage Company were delighted to employ a young man who could handle horses, guns, and had fought the rebels. The line from Hope all the way up to Hell's Mouth was a tough route. Jim Cotton was a tough boy. They liked him and he liked sitting up there on the board and not having to place one foot in front of the other, hour after hour, day after day, on the hard ground.

Jim Cotton thought back to those days now. Station 5, Laurie had said. It was the first relay station out of Hope. At Station 5 there was a route north and another towards

Hell's Mouth in the east. Back in his day the station had been nothing more than a single cabin with some stables out back. Teams of horses could be fed, watered, rested and changed, and passengers – never as important as the horses – could get some shade, and those heading north could rest up until their stage arrived. The station was fifteen miles out of Hope. A couple of rough hours on the coach; more on Molly, who was hot and tired. He'd need to get back to Hope and borrow a horse – if anyone in town was willing to lend him one. He'd become a pariah overnight. Amelia would be long gone from Station 5. He knew that. But maybe he could catch her at 4 or 3. If she made it to Hell's Mouth then the chances were she'd be staying overnight. He'd find her there and had no doubt that she'd come back with him. But the further east she was then the further it was back.

And Judge Wilkes was due to arrive in Hope tomorrow.

CHAPTER FIVE

At just gone midday, Pigeon Parker said, 'It'll be ten dollars, you're coming back today?'

Jim said, 'If I come back tomorrow it'll be too late.'

Pigeon said, 'They're the fastest I've got.'

'How soon can they be ready?'

'How soon do you want?'

'Now.'

'Give me fifteen minutes. Help yourself to coffee.' Pigeon nodded toward the stove.

The Hope Livery, run by Pigeon Parker but owned by some fellows who only ever made it west of the Mississippi once, was on the outskirts of town. It had been one of the first permanent buildings erected in Hope, and Jim Cotton wondered if the reason it was now on the edge of town was because folks had intentionally built upwind of the livery. The damp smell of manure and the dry scent of rat droppings filled the office. There was an acidity to the air, too. Rats again, Jim thought. He decided to pass on the coffee.

Fifteen minutes later he was heading east, pushing the

two horses hard, but aware that they had most probably a whole day of riding ahead of them. His own body felt older. Bruises from yesterday were coming out and his muscles and bones ached from that morning's kicking. But he pictured the fear in Sam's eyes and he saw again the rope tight around his neck, and his own physical pain vanished like raindrops on hot sand.

There hadn't been time to go and see Sam. He hadn't gone further than the Livery, leaving Molly there and taking two fast horses – one for him and one, pray God, for Amelia. He'd filled up a water bottle from a jug in Pigeon's office and was gone, back out into the scorching midday sun, the sky clear blue from Hope all the way to Hell's Mouth and beyond.

Station 5 had grown almost as much as McLean's ranch had grown. The original shack and staff bunkhouse had been knocked down and replaced by a stone building twice the size. There was a stable building out back, with a large corral. Next door to the station was a small hotel – a sign said *Whiskey and Beer! Beds. Piano.* Next door to that was another stone building with a sign offering *Baths, Shaves, and Good Food.* Two other buildings were in the process of being constructed – just wooden frames at the moment, but nestled within the timber skeletons were tents. A sign, lopsided and already fading in the fierce sunlight, proclaimed the area Black's Junction.

The vast changes made Jim Cotton realize how narrow his own life had become. For years he had toiled just a few miles down the road, rarely venturing beyond the Hope town limits. Now he saw how fast things were changing beyond those limits and somewhere deep inside he felt a sense of loss, but wasn't sure for what. Maybe, he thought, it was just for the way things had turned out in his own life.

He hitched the horses to the rail outside the stagecoach line office, and went inside.

The room was cool. Here, in the shadows, Jim felt his damp undershirt sticking to his skin, new sweat trickling down his flanks, a fresh dryness in his throat. On two sides of the room, and in the centre were wooden benches, currently empty. Oil lamps, unlit but still giving off the dark scent of kerosene, hung from a ceiling stained with the smoke from the lamps. At the far end was a counter, a barred window separating the clerk from anyone in the waiting room. There was a faint smell of rats in the place that made Jim think of Pigeon's place back along the trail.

He walked up to the counter. There was no one there.

'Hello?'

His voice sounded quiet and dry. Most of all it sounded old.

He heard someone sigh and put something down heavily on a table. A moment later a young man appeared at the window. The man looked scarcely older than Sam. His hair was greasy, his face pockmarked and pale. He wore a red waistcoat over a white shirt that had dirt at the collar and cuffs. Jin noticed a revolver over on the right side of the counter on the clerk's side.

'Afternoon,' Jim said.

' 'Noon.' The boy's eyes were red-rimmed. He yawned and despite the distance between them Jim caught the smell of stale whiskey. 'What can I do for you?'

43

'How long ago did the stage go through?'

The boy looked at him as if trying to figure something out.

'Which one?'

'How many are there?'

'North, east, and west,' the boy said.

'East.'

The boy reached into his vest pocket and pulled out a pocket watch. He flicked it open.

'Three-thirty,' he said. 'That's now.'

'OK. So. . . .'

'The coach left here right on time. Eleven o'clock.'

Over the years Jim Cotton had seen the stage leaving Hope, just along from Ben Garcia's office, so many times that it had almost become invisible to him, just another part of the scenery, the same as the church, the saloon, the hotel, and Irwin Foote's mercantile, the plank-walks and water troughs and everything else that you didn't see unless something wasn't right. For years he'd taken time out to talk to the drivers and to look over the coaches, to see how they'd improved them, made them more comfortable, but as his own driving days had receded even those conversations had lessened. He tried to recall now what time the stage left Hope and wasn't able to. His bones were aching and his arms and legs felt more tired more quickly than they used to. Who was to say your memory didn't go the same way?

'Eleven o'clock?' he said, trying to run calculations in his head as to how far away that meant they now might be.

'Eleven o'clock, sir.'

'And was there a girl on board?'

44

Now the boy ran his tongue out and over his lips. He tilted his head slightly to one side.

'A girl?'

'Yes, a girl A pretty girl. Maybe your age. I'm sure you'd have noticed her.'

The boy shook his head slowly, dreamily.

'There was no girl?' Jim said. He wanted to reach through the grille and shake some life into the boy.

'Might have been,' the boy said. 'I'm trying to remember.' He was still staring at Jim. Jim figured the kid was way too young to be losing his memory.

'Try harder, son.'

'You don't mean the north-bound stage, do you?'

Jim Cotton felt a tremor in his chest. If there had been a north-bound stage that morning, too, maybe Amelia had been on that one. If so, which one should he chase?

'What time did that one leave?'

'Not sure I recall.'

Jim turned, took a deep breath. On the wall opposite was a poster that looked, from this distance, like it might be a timetable.

'Should I go and read the times myself?' he said. 'Or are you going to help me?'

'Nine o'clock. Was running a little late.'

'And the girl?'

'The pretty girl?' the boy said, still shaking his head. Now he raised his thin eyebrows – suggesting a question that he didn't want to speak aloud.

Jim Cotton fumbled in his pocket. He brought out a small coin pouch, and from within it a silver dollar, then placed the coin on the counter on his side of the grille.

'The girl.'

'Ah yes, I think I recall a pretty girl.'

'Which way did she go?'

The boy nodded towards the dollar. Jim slid it beneath the grille. The boy picked it up, looked at it closely.

'*Who-eeh.* Another new one.'

'Which way?'

'East. She went east. Brought her ticket right here. Had a couple of fellows with her who wouldn't leave until they saw her on the coach.'

'That wasn't so hard, was it?'

'My memory was foggy for a moment, sir, that was all.'

'I need water for my horses. And for me.'

'Down alongside the hotel. They sank a well there. Who'd have thought there'd be water here. Was the Indians told us about it apparently.'

Jim turned and headed for the door. They were four hours ahead of him. Every second counted. He would water the horses and himself, and then, aching bones and bruised limbs aside, he'd push on.

'You from Hope?' the kid said, just as Jim was about to step back out into the blazing sunshine.

When Jim turned the boy wasn't looking at him, instead he was holding the silver dollar between his thumb and fore-finger, seemingly entranced by the way the sun came through the window and glinted off the coin.

'Where else is there to be from?'

'Lots of places,' the kid said.

'Why d'you ask?'

'You minting these down there?'

Jim shook his head.

46

'Second one I seen in as many days. I like a shiny coin, me.'

Now Jim paused. He'd noticed the coins, too. Not the way the kid had, not so entranced that he'd had trouble tearing his eyes away from Liberty or, on the other side, the eagle. But still it was nice to get a clean coin once in a while.

He'd been given it by Irwin Foote just a few days previously in exchange for sharpening some spades, saws, and knives for which Irwin had taken delivery.

'Who gave you the first one,' Jim said, walking back towards the boy. There must have been something in his voice or in his stance because this time the kid looked at him and didn't try to be smart and make him pay for information.

'I got it from Henry Herbert over at the hotel last night. He pays me, Henry. Was my wages. Couple of old coins and a nice new one.'

'Why did you ask if I came from Hope?'

'I said to Henry, that's a nice coin. Got any more like that. He said no. I asked him where he got it and he said a rider up from Hope that day – yesterday – had given it to him.'

'What did this rider look like?'

'I don't know. You'll have to ask Henry.'

'Is he there now?'

'Where else is there to be?'

Henry Herbert was an old man for the territories, maybe in his fifties, with a girth to frighten even the stoutest of horses. His face was red and what hair he had clustered about his ears like sage brush around a boulder. His eyes had the same tired look that had haunted the clerk's eyes next door, and when he walked he slightly dragged his right foot.

'The fellow was young,' Herbert said. 'No older than Joey over at the ticket hall.'

Jim Cotton sipped the beer that Herbert had poured for him. Least he could do, Jim had figured, was buy a beer. Doing so had, it appeared, made him Henry Herbert's best friend. He couldn't help but wonder how a fellow could grow to that size out here in the territories. Most people Jim knew always had the smell of hunger about them.

'Anything odd about him?' he asked.

Herbert frowned. 'How do you mean?'

'I don't know,' Jim said. It was probably nothing anyway. Nothing more than wishful thinking. 'Maybe in the way he was acting?'

'He calmed down after a while,' Herbert said. 'Does that help?'

'Calmed down?'

'After a few drinks.'

'Most people get worked up after a few drinks,' Jim said.

'Not this one. He looked scared. But after a while, like I said, he calmed down. It's good beer.' He smiled, lifted his own glass. 'Wouldn't you agree?'

'Best in Black's Junction.'

Herbert's smile widened. There was no need to say aloud that it was the only beer in Black's Junction. Real beer was a rare treat in the territory.

'What d'he look like, this kid?'

Herbert frowned again. 'Like I said, he was Joey's age.

Longish hair. Unwashed. Dusty clothes. What does anyone look like?'

'Would you recognize him again?'

'Sure I would. But why should I? What's going on here?'

'Three people got shot in Hope yesterday. Four actually. Three of them were shot dead, and the fourth may well have joined them by now. That kid look like he might be able to do such a thing?'

'I heard about the shooting,' Herbert said. His face, easy to smile and easy to frown, now took on a sad look. 'Some cowboys came up this morning with a girl for the stage. They said that a fellow had already been locked up for the killings. Figure you're chasing the wrong man if you've got your eyes on the kid who was here.'

Jim Cotton sipped the beer. It really did taste good. His throat and lips had been drier than he'd realized, that sun cooking him as slowly and surely as a hunk of rib-eye on a trail fire.

'Maybe,' he said. 'But maybe there's some doubt about it. Maybe the facts need to be put in front of the judge and let him decide. Maybe you'd be willing to tell him what you told me – you know, the kid being nervous and scared? About those silver dollars that matched the one I got from the store he robbed.'

'*If* he robbed it,' Herbert said. 'Anyway, from what those fellows were saying earlier it ain't going to be down to any judge.'

'What do you mean?'

'They was saying they're were heading back to Hope tonight and this time they were going to hang the boy the way they should have done yesterday.'

49

CHAPTER SIX

Jim Cotton stood in the baking sunshine, oblivious to the heat. He looked east, beyond the stage company offices and saw the trail snaking gently upwards until it disappeared over a rise. The hot wind blew sand against his face. He blinked and found tears in his eyes. The sand found its way into his mouth. He turned his back to the breeze and now found himself looking back the way he'd come, the hotel in front of him, and beyond it, blue sky, mountains, and somewhere a group of men gathering again to hang his only son for something he hadn't done.

He wiped his eyes, ran the damp hand over his lips. The horses had drunk their fill from the trough by the well. The beer had made him thirsty, rather than slaking any thirst. He lifted the ladle that was hooked on to the side of the well bucket and drank the cool water himself. It tasted metallic, but clean. He had an empty skin on the back of one of the horses. He filled it.

He turned and looked east again.

He'd made good time. He pushed the horses a little too hard, swapping over from one to the other every half hour. But they were sleek, well muscled, and strong and he had confidence that he'd catch the stage before it reached Hell's Mouth – where Amelia could catch the Atchison, Topeka and Santa Fe and be gone forever. Hs own body was a different matter. He ached terribly, and there was increasing pain in his hips and in his arms. His neck clicked when he turned his head and his eyes were sore. His sight was blurred from the brightness and now he realized there was a permanent whistling in his ears.

When there had been no choice none of this mattered. He would chase down Amelia and bring her home. She would tell the truth and Sam would be released.

But now . . . now he had to go home. Now he had to warn Benito and Hector what was being planned. Now he had to stand side by side with them once again and fight off the mob once more. Yet if he did that, where did that get him? Tomorrow Judge Wilkes would arrive and without Amelia's testimony Sam would hang anyway.

So he had to go on – he had to reach Amelia and hope that her love for Sam was enough of a pull to turn her around and make her ride back to Hope with him. Hell, if she wasn't prepared to come willingly then he'd bring her anyway. One way or the other she was coming home.

But then he saw once more the rope dropping from the roof of Benito's office and the cowboy up there winding it around a beam and someone down on the plank-walk pulling it tight around Sam's neck.

He looked up at the sky, at the sun that was already tracking towards the mountains. He opened his mouth in a silent scream, screwed up his face in pain, clenched his fist, then he asked God for help.

There was no answer.

51

He thought back to the days of his youth. The fear of battle, of killing, of being killed, moments when he was so scared that he couldn't ever imagine life throwing anything worse at him, up there in the rocks at Glorieta Pass, knowing that those were the worst hours of his life.

He'd been wrong. This helplessness was worse. Being an old man in the middle of nowhere not knowing which way to go, suspecting that the wrong choice would see Sam die.

Knowing that either choice might see Sam die.

'Think,' he said aloud. 'You've not come this far for nothing, Jim Cotton.'

Across the street, if the cleared and rutted space between hotel, stage office, and bath-house could be called a street, a man came out of Herbert's Hotel and walked across to where the wooden frames of the new buildings rose up. The man crouched down and went inside one of the tents that were set within the timber framework.

The reality was, Jim thought, that he had been hopeless yesterday in front of the sheriff's office. All it had taken was a couple of younger guys to knock him over and hold him down and he'd been helpless. The thought brought with it a dark feeling of sadness, despair almost, at how impotent he'd been. His boy had been facing eternity and he'd been face down in the dirt. And what was to say it would be any different today? He could give up chasing Amelia and end up being helpless back in Hope again.

What he could do, what he had to do, was warn Benito what was being planned – what McLean was planning. At least that way Benito could make some arrangements, whatever they might be, to protect Sam.

Jim Cotton walked back across the street and into the

hotel again.

Henry Herbert looked up from a ledger in which he was painstakingly printing tiny capital letters.

'Couldn't resist another beer? I thought you'd be well on your way by now,' Herbert said. 'Wherever that might be.'

'I ought to be. But what you said earlier got me to thinking.'

'What did I say, friend?'

'That the fellows who were here this morning were planning on lynching my – that boy back in Hope.'

'Yep.'

'Tell me, is there a good man in town? I mean, here, at the Junction.'

'A good man for what?'

'I need to get a message to the sheriff in Hope about what you said, and I'm going in the other direction.'

Herbert nodded. For a moment Jim thought the big man was going to offer to go himself. He hoped not. There wouldn't be a horse in the country could carry that man anywhere fast or far.

'There's a couple of guys about.'

'Will one of them do it?'

'It's a quiet day.'

'I'll pay.'

'How much you got?'

Jim Cotton pulled his coin pouch from his pocket.

'Two dollars.'

'It ain't much.'

'It's all I've got.'

It would still leave another of those bright new silver

dollars from Irwin's store. But he wanted to keep that one back. It wasn't evidence exactly, but when he came to explain that part of the story to Judge Wilkes – *if* he came to be able to explain that part of the story to Judge Wilkes – he wanted to have the coin in his hand. At least it would go some way to making the story real.

'What do you want this fellow to say?'

'I want him to tell Sheriff Benito Garcia that McLean's men are coming again for Sam. Tonight. If Benito isn't about, tell his deputy, Hector Lopez.'

Herbert said, 'Benito Garcia. McLean, Sam. And Hector Lopez.'

'Yes. It's important.'

Herbert scribbled something down in the margin on the edge of his ledger. 'OK,' he said.

'There's someone who'll do it?'

'What was your name again, mister?'

'Jim Cotton.'

'I'll get it done, Jim.'

The late afternoon's riding was much harder than any riding he'd already done that day. It was partly weariness, partly hunger – although he chewed on dry beef as he rode, washed down with the metallic tasting water from the Black's Junction well – but mostly it was down to fear. Fear that Herbert's man mightn't get to Hope in time and, even if he did, there might be nothing Ben and Hector could do about it. Fear that he mightn't catch up with the stagecoach. Fear that even if he did Amelia would refuse to come back. Fear that even if she did agree to return to Hope, would they have enough time to get there?

On numerous occasions he almost turned back, still not sure that the decision to continue to chase Amelia and her testimony was the right one.

He was also aware that he was pushing his horses too hard over ground that he knew from experience was dangerous both for its grades, ruts, and loose surface and because of where it was – outlaw country; Indian country. Back in his day there had often been three of them riding the stage, two up front, one at the back on a horse. All armed with shotguns and pistols. Even with such firepower there had been plenty of terrifying moments.

Then he topped a long grade and instantly pulled the horses to a halt, his heart hammering.

Ahead of him the stagecoach stood motionless in a natural rock cutting. All four horses were still tethered to the bars. The stagecoach doors were open. On the ground to the right lay two men. Several cases and boxes were on the ground, too. They had been opened – or had come open when thrown off the roof of the stagecoach – and brightly coloured clothes and shoes and some books were spread across the dirt. A violin case had split open, too, and the polished wood of the instrument reflected the low sun. One time, a lifetime ago it seemed, as a young soldier, Jim Cotton had heard a quartet of violin players performing a piece that had originated in Europe. He couldn't recall (maybe had never known) who the composer had been but the music had been beautiful, twisting and turning, not like a mean rattlesnake, but like a beautiful serene river. The violin lying in the shadow of the stagecoach had suffered a broken neck.

Jim Cotton reached behind and slid his Spencer rifle

from its scabbard. He ran his eyes over the rocks, both high and low, either side of the trail. He sat still and let peripheral vision alert him to any movement.

There was none, save the circling of several buzzards high above him.

After long enough for the shadows on the ground to have moved several inches and for his heart to return to its normal rate he lightly squeezed his heels into the horse's flanks and edged her forwards.

He scanned the rocks and shadows as he approached the stagecoach, but he knew the men who had done this were long gone. It was too quiet. And now, looking down at the first of the men on the ground, he saw that not only had he been shot, but someone had also cut his throat. It looked like the buzzards had been at him, too, and they wouldn't have done that if there had still been people around.

Both men's blood had dried and soaked into the ground, but there was still a metallic tang in the air. It reminded Jim of the water from Black's Junction and he wondered if he'd be able to drink any more of it no matter how hard his thirst.

He circled the stagecoach. There was a third body on the far side. An older man. Not so much blood this time.

Jim Cotton held his breath and listened. One of the horses tethered to the stagecoach snorted. He could hear his own horse breathing.

Other than that there was nothing.

He ran his eyes over the rocks again. No one there either.

No one but him.

Most of all, no Amelia McLean.

CHAPTER SEVEN

Skunk McLean sat on the top railing of the fence and said, 'He damn near raped Amelia. To be honest, I think he may actually have raped her.' He looked at his men gathered outside the bunkhouse in the early evening sunlight. A few of them had been in town the day before when Sam Cotton had almost been hanged – in fact Skunk had made sure of it. If no one from town had shown any inclination to hang the boy then his men would have stoked that particular fire. All of his men had thus now heard about the incident. They were good men. Tough, rough and, as often as they could be, pretty wild. But good. And he could see in their eyes that they wanted to do the right thing by Amelia, and by the poor folks in town who had been murdered by Sam Cotton.

OK, maybe he was being a little loose with the truth around the rape, but sure as silver that boy would have done so sooner or later.

'If any of you don't want to come,' he said, 'that's OK. I won't hold it against you.'

'We're all behind you, boss,' the one called Mitchell

said. A murmur of agreement went up from all of them.

'Just saying. If anyone wants to wait for Judge Wilkes.'

'Let's hang him tonight,' someone said.

'I appreciate your support. I know Amelia does, too.'

'What's the plan, boss?' a cowboy asked.

'We'll wait until an hour after dark and then set off for town. Let's keep it simple. We'll demand they hand the boy over to us.'

'Garcia's a good man. He won't just hand the kid over,' the same cowboy said.

McLean paused. He reached down and slipped the riding crop from his boot, the feel of it in his hand giving him a sense of command.

'Yes, I know. But then it'll be his call. You understand what I'm saying? You understand what might happen?'

'There might be some shooting.'

'Maybe. Though I think Ben will see our point of view if it comes right down to the wire.'

'And the kid's father?'

'He won't see our point of view, no matter what.'

'So what do we do?'

'We do whatever's necessary,' McLean said. 'I suspect to hang the son we're going to have to shoot the father.'

The stagecoach horses were dehydrated, their tongues smacking against dry lips. They were agitated too, panic in their eyes and restlessness in their legs. Jim Cotton unbuckled them from their harnesses and coaxed them away from the pole, and although they whinnied and stamped their hoofs they appeared reluctant to move away from the familiarity of the coach. He didn't have enough water for one let alone all four but they looked strong. They would be OK.

With the horses loose and able to fend for themselves, he turned his attention to the fact that there were three dead men on the ground and no sign of Amelia. He walked slowly along the trail staring at the ground. There were plenty of tracks but none that meant much to him. He knew a couple of Apaches who would have been able to read those tracks as well as he could read the Bible, probably better, but that didn't help him right now.

Further along the trail individual tracks became clearer but still hard to read, the dust and rock not showing up anything more than vague indentations and scratch marks.

He retraced his steps to the abandoned stagecoach. There were less tracks heading back the way he had come. So, whoever it was had hit the stagecoach and gone back the same way. It wasn't much, but it was all he had.

He climbed back on to his horse and nudged her slowly along the trail, his eyes scanning the ground one moment then looking up at the rocks on either side of the trail. He sensed that whoever had robbed the stage and killed those three men was long gone – but there was no point in taking chances. Back at Glorieta he had seen what happened to men who got caught open in a pass.

A few hundred yards further on the rocks on either side started to flatten out. There was more grass, even some stunted trees, and it was along the side of one of these trees that the scuffed tracks led.

He stopped.

The sun cast long shadows now. In an hour or two it

would be too dark to read the ground even in his limited fashion. Despair swept over him. Amelia was out there somewhere – maybe dead, but more probably not, he thought. If they – whoever *they* were – had been going to shoot her they would have done so back at the stagecoach with those other three. No, she was a pretty girl. These were desperate men. She might wish she were dead, though. Without Amelia his whole plan was ruined. Without Amelia Sam would hang. And looking out over the open ground, the clusters of trees and rocks, the grasses and the cacti and the distant mountains, it felt like an impossible task to find them, let alone rescue the girl and get home, all before dawn.

He closed his eyes, both to pray and for relief against the dry dust. On his retinas he again saw the image of a man on the sheriff's office roof throwing down a rope.

He opened his eyes.

What would those Apache trackers do?

What they *wouldn't* do, was give up, he knew that. Even now, after forty years of fighting and after almost all hope was gone they were still out there battling to save their land and their families and their history. Battling to save their own. No matter how high the odds.

Save their own.

That was what he had to do. He hadn't fought wars and survived the elements and hewn out an existence on the frontier just to give up. The deaths of his loved ones would not be in vain. Whilst there was still breath in him – and breath still in Sam – he would fight on.

There was blood on the ground.

At first he had thought it was just a dark shadow on a

pale stone. But now he saw that it was blood. He jumped to the ground, reached out and touched it. It was dry. But that meant little. Blood dried quickly. Hell, in this heat rivers dried quickly.

He scanned the ground in front of him.

Nothing.

He took a few paces along the route where he best-guessed the men had ridden and suddenly he could see where the grass was crushed.

Another few paces, still walking, still leading his two horses.

More blood.

And now he had a line – two patches of dropped blood, crushed grass – and he stood straight and followed the line with his eyes. In the distance the ground rose up gently, and then more steeply. He could see a group of trees that looked healthy enough to suggest nutrition and water. Beyond the trees, in the rocks and the hills there would a hundred places to hide.

That's where they would be.

They would have put as much distance between them and the stagecoach as they could. But they were only a few hours ahead of him and they would be slowed by the girl. They would want to camp before dark. And they would all want to use the girl.

He climbed back on the horse and set out along the line that he had plotted. Discovering those few clues – almost as if he was channeling the skills of people who had lived here for centuries – had given him a renewed energy.

An hour later, on four huge slabs of rock that formed a series of steps up a particular steep rise, he saw more blood.

It felt as if something was guiding him, helping him. The feeling gave him hope, and he pushed on, faster now.

More trees rose up around him, although they were still sparse enough that when the land opened out he could see for many miles. The sun was sinking over his shoulder, the shadows almost as long as they would ever get, and the evening chill was rising. The ache in his bones and in his muscles had become permanent, but he scarcely noticed pain. He was hungry and thirsty. His eyes were sore and when he breathed he felt the sand all the way down inside his lungs. He still swapped horses every hour, his own tiredness less important to him than that of the horses. When darkness fell, that previous despair tried to sweep over him once more. This time he immediately fought against it, refusing to give up, telling himself again that something was guiding him. From somewhere came the idea that it wasn't ancient Indians, but that it was Mary, Sam's mother, doing this guiding. Although, whilst believing this, he was also aware enough of his own situation to wonder if he wasn't starting to hallucinate. Last night he had only slept in fits and starts and today he had spent the entire day in the saddle under a blazing sun with little food. Two physical beatings in two days didn't even come close to what he had suffered emotionally.

He topped a rise, his horse slipping slightly on loose stones that neither he nor the horse could see.

And, about two miles ahead, he saw the flickering light of a fire.

'Thank you, Mary,' he said.

Jim Cotton left the horses half a mile or so away from

where the men were camping. He took a knife from one saddle-bag, slipped it carefully into his belt, held his Spencer in his right hand, and began to work his way forwards.

The moon was large, not quite full yet, but bright enough that he was able to find darker shadows to move between. He thought back to his days training as a soldier. There'd been nothing like this. No edging forwards this slowly, almost motionless, minute by minute. What there had been was violence and bullying and men trying to break boys in order to build them back up and prepare them for what might happen to them. Jim Cotton could still feel some of those lessons deep inside although he wasn't sure he could be specific about what they had entailed any more. It had been too long ago and this day had been too long. He was hungry and thirsty and he ached in every muscle. He was tired and his eyes were sore and whenever he blinked there was a huge temptation to keep his eyelids closed. But beneath it all there was the knowledge that he had to save Sam, and to do that he had to get Amelia.

So he crawled on, aware of the harsh sound of his own breathing, and the rattle of stones beneath his legs. When he heard the gang's horses he crawled around a wide loop to avoid them.

As he neared the camp the sound of the girl sobbing came to him on the still night air. He stopped. A man was talking to her, talking dirty. He heard the man grunt and groan, heard Amelia plead with him. He heard a slap, and Amelia cried out in pain and hopelessness.

Then, about six feet from where he was lying, someone

stood up – Jim Cotton had thought the shape in front of him was just a large rock. The man turned and looked back towards the camp.

'Don't you be spoiling her,' he called. 'I want my turn.'

'There's enough to go round,' somebody replied.

'There'd better be,' the man said, then turned back to look out towards the distant dark trail.

Jim Cotton lay still. He hadn't formulated a plan other than to get close enough to see what was what and to somehow play it by ear. The fact they'd placed a guard – at least one – made things a little more difficult. But it didn't change anything. He still had to get Amelia away from these men.

Whatever it took.

The man lifted a bottle to his lips, emptied it, and threw the bottle out into the darkness.

'How's it going back there?' he asked.

Amelia was crying now.

'She needs comforting,' someone said. 'Come and see if you can cheer her up, Meredith. Sam, you go and keep a watch.'

'Ain't nobody coming,' the one called Sam said. Sam, Jim thought. The same name. It felt like a fist had just closed around his heart.

'Well it'll be an easy job then, won't it?'

Meredith, the man who had been on guard, had already started making his way towards the camp. Jim Cotton took the opportunity to roll deeper in to the darkness where stunted trees and wild brush were growing. He lay still, and without realizing he'd drawn it, he found the knife in his hand.

The one called Sam came out of the darkness swigging on his own whiskey bottle. As he passed the first guard he said, 'She's mighty pretty, Mer'. Be having me some more later on.'

Then he sat on the rock where Meredith had been, humming quietly to himself and drinking at regular intervals.

Jim Cotton wondered how often these men were planning on changing their watch and whether they were disciplined enough to keep it up all night long. He needed the men asleep. Only then could he sneak in and get Amelia out of there.

Yet the clock was ticking. The moon was tracking across the night sky and somewhere Judge Wilkes was getting closer. There was a faint glimmer of hope in Jim Cotton's mind that perhaps Judge Wilkes was heading in from Hell's Mouth and would come across the abandoned stagecoach and the bodies. But so what if he did? Maybe it would just make him even more angry and determined to hand out the harshest punishments he could when murderers were brought before him. Or maybe he was coming in from the north anyway, meeting the Hope trail at Station 5. Whichever way you looked at it, come the morrow Sam would be on trial for his life, and here Jim Cotton daren't move until these outlaws had had their fill of whiskey and Amelia.

She screamed. The scream tailed off into a wail, then a sob. Several men laughed. The one called Sam took a long swig from his bottle, looked back over his shoulder, belched, and then slid down off the rock. He carefully – drunkenly – placed the bottle on the ground and, unbuttoning his trousers, walked towards where Jim Cotton was lying.

Then he was standing right above Jim letting out a long stream of hot urine. It splashed on Jim Cotton's face and although he knew all he had to do was lie still and within a minute it would be over he couldn't help but try and move backwards a few inches.

'What's that?' Sam said, stepping forward, still urinating. 'Possum?'

Jim Cotton had killed men in the war, but it had never been close up. Now it felt as if someone else was inhabiting his body, the aches and pains and tiredness, the grittiness in his eyes and the dryness in his mouth all vanished and there was a feeling that he could do anything, no matter how old his bones, no matter that he believed in God, no matter that this boy had the same name as his own boy. These men had killed the stagecoach crew and the male passengers and were right now raping Amelia. Jim Cotton figured that God was surely on his side.

The outlaw was buttoning his trousers, walking round the bush, edging into the darkness of the trees looking for whatever had made the noise.

'Here, little rabbit,' Sam said, and Jim Cotton rose up behind him, grabbed him around the head with his left arm, clamping his left hand over the boy's mouth, and with his right drawing his knife sharply and deeply across the boy's throat. He felt hot blood spurt out of the wound and the kid jack-knifed violently. Jim Cotton held him until he stopped moving and then he stepped deeper into the shadows, dragging the body as far out of sight as he could.

The kid had a six-gun in his belt. Jim Cotton took it, along with a handful of cartridges from his belt.

He spat on the ground but the taste of a dead man's urine was still in his mouth. He wiped his sleeve across his face but the sleeve was soaked with blood. He stood there, covered in the boy's fluids, his own heart hammering, breath coming too fast, a hard knot growing in his belly and he knew he was going to be sick.

He vomited as quietly as he could but still someone yelled out, 'I told you that whiskey was only for real men.'

Jim Cotton retched again, and in the camp several men laughed.

From the way the moon and stars were placed, and from the way the cold was starting to make his bones physically hurt, Jim Cotton figured it was sometime around two in the morning when one of the outlaws staggered out of the camp to relieve the one called Sam, only to find the boy was nowhere to be found.

CHAPTER EIGHT

Earlier, at around eleven o'clock, Skunk McLean rode into Hope with almost twenty-five hands. He could have brought thirty-five – every one of his men was fired-up and looking to be part of the lynch mob – but he had insisted on leaving some back at the ranch to guard the place. He wasn't overly worried about the last few Apaches – he had a deal with them that involved whiskey and horses – but he had learned the hard way that you shouldn't ever turn your back on them.

The twenty-five men who had ridden with him were liquored up and looking for blood.

As they rode into Hope he saw the few people on the moonlit plank-walk stop and stare. In a couple of buildings curtains were pulled aside and people looked out. As the mob rode by several men staggered out from the Domino saloon to see what the noise was about.

'Trouble,' one of the drinkers said, his face yellow in the light of a kerosene lamp hanging outside the saloon door.

'Skunk's middle name,' his companion replied.

The mob pulled up their horses outside the sheriff's office and jail.

'They've come back for the Cotton kid,' another drinker said. His words were relayed inside the saloon and within seconds most people who had been inside came out to watch the moonlit figures.

McLean raised a hand and his boys brought their horses under control. Just the occasional snort and whinny and stamping of a foot drifted across the town on the cold night air.

Further along the street, from the window in her room above the schoolhouse, Tessa Brown looked out. It took her just a few seconds to realize what was happening. She saw how this time – unlike last – the townsfolk weren't part of the mob. This time they were just spectators – a crowd over there by the Domino, several groups of people up and down the plank-walk, a cluster forming across the square by the church, all of them keeping their distance, keeping out of it. This time not wanting to be part of whatever was going to happen. That was bad. There was no sign of Raoul Vega or Martha Kane, but even if there had been, Tessa thought, they could have done nothing. Those men on horses weren't from the town, they wouldn't listen to Raoul or Martha's pleadings.

Tessa watched a moment longer. She heard the man at the head of the lynch mob call for Sheriff Benito Garcia to come out and to bring the goddamn keys if he knew what was good for him.

Ben Garcia never appeared.

The man called for him again, saying if Garcia didn't come out then they were coming in. Several of the men were reaching for their guns now. Tessa saw that one of the riders had a long coil of rope over his shoulder. He was easing it over his head now, holding the rope in his hands, caressing it.

Still there was no sign of Garcia.

She turned away from the window, grabbed a white woollen shawl that she had knitted herself, and hurried down the stairs and outside.

Not for one second did she imagine that she could stop these men doing what they had come to do, but she knew she wouldn't ever be able to look Jim Cotton in the eye again if she didn't at least try.

In the square Skunk McLean said, 'Don't look like they're coming out, boys.' He swung off his horse. Another half-a-dozen men did the same.

'Let's go get him.'

The outlaw said, 'Sammy? Where you at, son? You ready for another go, or are you all worn out?'

Jim Cotton held his breath.

'Kid?' The man sounded weary. 'Where are you?'

He walked out along the trail a little ways then came back, did a circuit of the big rock that they had chosen as the guard post, came to the edge of the trees and the wild bushes in which Jim Cotton had retreated further and in which the body of the kid called Sam was already getting cold.

The man's feet crunched on stones and dried twigs but it was too dark to see him.

'Kid, you asleep?'

The man pushed forward into the brush.

'Kid?'

Another few steps, Jim thought, and if he didn't see the body he was sure to step on it.

'You gone back in for some more already?' the man said. 'Sonofabitch.'

Jim Cotton held the knife tightly in his hand. He'd spent an hour trying to come to terms with the fact that he'd killed a man, a young man, a boy with the same name as his own son. An hour hadn't been long enough. The way he felt he didn't know if he'd ever come to terms with it. It felt as if everything he had ever stood for, ever believed in, ever valued, had been wiped out with that single knife stroke. At the same time, he had told himself over and over, he was like a cornered animal fighting for his life, like a bitch fighting to protect her pups. It was nature. Of course, the argument hadn't worked. He still felt as desperate, lonely, and evil as he had ever felt in his life.

But he knew if this fellow took another step forward then he'd cut *his* throat as surely as he had done the kid's.

'Garcia,' McLean said, halfway up the steps to the office door. 'Last chance, Sheriff.' He was climbing the steps as he spoke. 'Nothing against you, Sheriff. We just want the boy.'

Tessa Brown ran across the square.

'Stop!' she cried.

Nobody paid her any attention.

'Stop!'

A few people looked across at her, but she was too little too late – McLean and a couple of hands had now gone

71

inside the office.

Tessa ran between the cowhands who were still outside on their horses. An oil lantern was burning inside the sheriff's office, some light coming out of his door, and the moon was close to being full. But still the men outside were faceless dark beings. A horse whinnied next to her. She put one foot on to the steps outside the sheriff's office and someone grabbed her from behind.

'Get off me,' she said.

'Uh-huh,' the man said. 'You wait outside, lady.'

'Let me go!'

'You don't want to see this.'

She tried to twist out of his grasp but his hands were tight on her arms.

'This is evil. You know it's evil.'

'The boy is evil, lady.'

'He deserves a fair trial!'

'He deserves what he's going to get.'

'Let me—'

A shot rang out from inside Ben Garcia's office.

The outlaw stopped – just a footfall or two away from the kid's body. 'Kid, I don't know where you've got to,' he said, the words slurring together. Then he turned and made his way back to the rock, where he sat silhouetted against the moon. Jim Cotton breathed a sigh of relief, but it was tempered with anxiety. Time was moving on. His bones were getting increasingly cold. The moon was crawling relentlessly across the sky. He needed to get into the camp, and get Amelia out of there. He needed to return to Hope.

Jim still wasn't exactly sure how far away the camp was. It was close – he could still hear Amelia crying softly now and then – but noise travelled a long way on the night air.

He waited a while longer and watched the man on the rock shift around trying to get comfortable. It might have been Jim's imagination or wishful thinking, but once or twice he was sure the man's chin dropped a little as he fought against sleep.

Eventually Jim knew he had no choice. Time had run too far, his bones and body were seizing up. He had to make his move.

He slipped the knife into his boot and the six-gun into his waistband and eased himself forwards, staying within the tree line – for what it was worth – crawling, taking every inch slowly, working around the back of rocks and bushes, stopping and listening every few seconds. He let the girl's cries lead him. He heard several people snoring, he heard the snort of horses. Someone muttered something, but it sounded like they were talking in their sleep. Jim could taste dirt and cold sand on his lips, smell the fresh earth and the wild grass, smell smoke . . . and then he was on the edge of their camp, looking across at the embers of the fire, seeing one, two, three . . . five men, maybe six, laid out under their blankets.

Across the camp was Amelia.

She was awake, but it was impossible for him to signal to her. As best Jim could tell in the darkness she was bound by her hands to a tree on the far side of the camp. She was wearing a white blouse that looked torn and dirty in the moonlight, and was curled up, her legs beneath her, her head down.

He eased backwards into the undergrowth and worked his way slowly around towards her.

'Where is he?' Skunk McLean demanded, his gun was sill smoking. 'Where in the hell is he?'

Ben Garcia sat rocked back in his chair, feet up on his desk.

'I once met Billy the Kid,' he said. 'Bill Bonney, you heard of him? You might know him as Bill Antrim. Maybe another name, no? Billy had a lot of names.'

'Where's the Cotton boy?' McLean said.

'Everyone said you couldn't reason with Billy,' Ben Garcia said. 'That he was crazy.'

'What are you talking about?'

When they had burst into the office Garcia had been sitting there, seemingly asleep, but actually as wide awake as he had ever been. He had opened his eyes lazily but hadn't shown the slightest surprise. A shotgun lay across his lap. The door to the room which held the cages had been locked. When he had politely refused to unlock the door and bring out Sam Cotton, McLean had drawn his own gun and shot the lock off. A moment later McLean had discovered two of the cages were empty, and in the third it was the horse thief Floyd Casey, not Sam Cotton.

'See, I think I can reason with you, that you're a *reasonable* man,' Garcia said.

'What have you done with the Cotton boy?'

'Whereas Billy, you never knew. He was the nicest kid you could meet. But he was like a snake. He could turn on you, you know?'

McLean said, 'I'm no more reasonable than a snake

74

myself.' He pointed his gun at Garcia. 'Where have you put him?'

'We've been through this. Yesterday. We agreed we'd wait for Wilkes. It won't be long now. He's due tomorrow.'

'We're not waiting.'

McLean pulled back the hammer on his Colt. 'Last chance, Sheriff.'

There were six of McLean's men in the room now. Outside Garcia could hear a woman shouting. Through the open door to the cages he could see Floyd, the horse thief, standing up, hands gripping the bars, trying to work out what was going on.

Garcia let his chair down gently. He sat up straight and slowly turned the shotgun towards McLean.

'*Uno*, McLean,' he said. 'You shoot me you better kill me straight away and hope I don't squeeze the trigger as I die. If I was a betting man I'd say we'd both die. *Dos*, you kill a sheriff you're going to hang too, no? Even if I don't kill you. That is, 'less you going to shoot Floyd, too, to cover up your crime.'

McLean looked through the cell door towards Floyd. It was dark in there but they all saw Floyd release his hands from the bars and hold them up in the air. 'I di'n't hear nothing,' he said. 'Honest I di'n't.'

'Fact is,' Garcia said. 'If you do kill him how you going to explain the shooting of an unarmed man locked in a cage?

'And *tres*, everybody who's still awake has seen you ride in and they all know what this is about. So—'

A woman burst into the room.

Garcia recognized her, the schoolteacher. One of

McLean's cowboys was right beside her. Blood was pouring from his nose. 'She elbowed me,' he said.

'You stop!' the woman said, looking from one face to another. The room was dim, lit by just that one lantern. Several moths fluttered around the flame. All the faces were dark and shadowed but she finally settled on McLean. 'You have no right—'

'Don't worry, Sam's gone, Miss. . . ?' Garcia said.

She looked at him, puzzlement in her eyes 'Brown, Tessa Brown. Where has he gone?'

McLean said, 'The sheriff was just about to tell us.'

'Just gone. He'll be back when the judge is ready and I'm not about to tell these men anything.'

Tessa thought about this for a moment and Garcia saw her start to smile. He said, 'These gentlemen were just working out why it's not a good idea to shoot me. Aside from the fact it would get them nowhere as regards Sam Cotton's whereabouts, it would almost certainly get them hanged.'

McLean stared at Garcia for a moment longer. 'We'll find him,' he said. 'If we have to tear this town apart building by building tonight, we'll find him.' He looked at one of his men. 'Start with the blacksmith's shop. That's where the boy lived. His father'll be there. He'll know where they've put the kid.'

'Why do you want the boy dead so quickly?' Garcia asked. 'Why won't you wait?'

'Cotton's shop,' McLean said to his men. 'Let's go.'

Jim Cotton slid forward and clamped his hand hard over Amelia McLean's mouth. Her eyes widened in fear. He could see the moon reflected in them.

'Shush,' he whispered. 'I'm a friend.'

Still her eyes were wide with terror.

'Jim Cotton,' he said. 'Sam's father.'

It took her a while to make the connection. Jim figured the experiences of the last few hours had caused her to withdraw to some dark and remote place in her mind and she was now having trouble finding her way back out of that darkness. Eventually there was something akin to recognition in her eyes. He could feel the breath from her nose coming hot and fast on to the back of his hand. She smelled of fear and blood.

'Don't scream or we're all dead. You, me, and . . . and Sam.'

His face was level with her own.

'Do you understand?'

She nodded.

'Sure?'

Nod.

'I'm going to remove my hand. Don't make a sound.'

Jim Cotton kept his hand pressed on Amelia's mouth a little longer. He was suddenly scared to remove it. If she shouted or screamed or even gasped noisily for air they'd both be dead. Sam, too.

She looked at him and nodded again.

He removed his hand and she did gasp for air, but she did it silently, her chest heaving, her mouth wide open.

He let her catch her breath, then he drew the knife from his boot.

'I'm going to cut you free,' he said. 'Once I've done that I want you to crawl behind me as quietly as you can.'

She nodded, and he crawled further into the camp, into the dying light of the fire under the bright moon and began sawing at her bonds.

Tessa Brown stood alongside Benito Garcia on the top of the wooden steps outside his office and watched the pandemonium unfold. It felt strange to be standing up there next to the sheriff – Jim Cotton had been there the day before, side by side with Ben and Hector, and now here she was. It gave her a feeling of closeness to Jim that she reluctantly understood was almost certainly only wishful thinking.

One of McLean's men came out of Jim Cotton's blacksmith shop and said the place was empty, neither the old man or the kid was there. McLean turned to Garcia and accused him of letting them go. Garcia told McLean that he had no idea where Jim Cotton was, but Sam Cotton would be present at the trial whenever that was to be.

Several of McLean's riders went into the Domino saloon. One of them came out trading punches with someone. It was too dark and they were too far away for Tessa to see who it was.

McLean's men went into the church and came out empty handed. They knocked on doors and threatened people. They searched the stagecoach office and they broke open the door to the mercantile where all the trouble had started. McLean sent two men up to the livery stables and directed several more to check out the alleyways and outhouses, hen-houses, smoke-houses, and dog-houses.

Within twenty minutes any goodwill or support that

McLean may have had for his form of frontier justice had evaporated. There were more fisticuffs, there were stand-offs with guns, and there were several warning shots fired.

Tessa Brown said to Benito Garcia, 'How did you know?'

'How did I know what?'

'That they would be coming back to try and lynch Sam again?'

'*Un pajarito me dijo,*' he said.

'A little bird told you?'

'You speak Spanish?'

'Just a little.'

'I don't know where Jim Cotton is,' Garcia said, 'but he's up to something, and someone rode in earlier to pass on a message from him. It's a good job they did. Please excuse me,' he said, stepping down into the street and checking the cartridge in his shotgun. 'It's time I put an end to all of this, no?'

In the moonlight Jim Cotton watched tears roll down Amelia's bruised and dirt-blackened face.

'It'll be all right,' he whispered, not sure he even believed the words himself.

She looked at him. Her eyes, dark with pain and awful experience, now seemed to suck in the moonlight without reflecting it. She opened her mouth to say something but she was unable to form words.

'Keep going,' he said, his words scarcely louder than the breath from his dry and cracked lips.

They were outside the perimeter of the camp. They'd worked their way back into the trees and bushes and were now slowly edging around the camp and towards safety. Jim Cotton knew they still had to be careful of the man on guard, but figured there was a good chance he might even be asleep now. Once beyond him they would make it to the horses and then it was just a case of getting home. They mightn't do it by dawn, but they would be there soon after, maybe mid-morning, possibly noon. It would be all right, he told himself. It *had* to be all right.

He started picturing the judge, imagining the setting up of the temporary court – probably in the town hall, which was just a room built on to the side of the hotel at the moment. Plans had been drawn up for a proper town hall – three storeys, made of brick – but so far the money hadn't been forthcoming. The word was that there were investors back East who were prepared to finance it but wanted something in return. If the town could persuade the Atchison, Topeka and Santa Fe Railway to extend the tracks all the way to Hope and the eastern businessmen could come up with a deal then maybe the town hall would be—

Amelia snatched the knife from the waistband of Jim's trousers, stood up, and started to scream.

She burst into the outlaws' camp and before any of the men had even begun to untangle themselves from their saddle blankets she drove the knife into one of them over and over again, his screams mixing with hers.

CHAPTER NINE

Samuel Cotton said from within the cave, 'I'm cold.'

The words weren't aimed at Hector Lopez who was sat at the mouth of the cave, but instead were just a statement of fact spoken in a flat and resigned voice, immediately snatched away by the night wind, and cast into the vast night sky.

From where he sat huddled up, a blanket wrapped around him, Sam could see stars stretching away – they went on forever, it seemed. The more he stared at them the more appeared. As a child, his mother had told him that every star was a person who had once lived, that when someone died then, providing they'd lived a good life, they would become a star.

He no longer believed his mother's explanation, but he couldn't help thinking on it – and on her – and he wondered what she would have said to him right now. She would have been able to help, he was sure. She would have made everything all right. A tear rolled down his cheek.

Maybe before he had chance to view the stars again then he too would be one of them.

'You want me to light a fire?' Hector said, not moving, not turning to look at Sam. 'Let everyone know where we are?'

'I'll stay cold.'

'It's better than dying.'

They'd heard gunshots earlier. The town was a long way away on the plain, and the shots had been faint.

'I'm sorry,' Sam said.

'For what?'

'For causing you all this trouble. For making you spend a night freezing.'

'I'm not cold.'

'For getting you hurt.'

'It was nothing. Horses have hurt me worse.'

'Anyway, I'm sorry.'

'I'm just doing my job. The town pays me and here I am.'

'What happens if someone comes up?'

'They won't.'

'But if they do. Amelia said—'

Now Hector turned towards Sam, his head silhouetted against the night sky.

'Amelia said what?'

'Amelia said that her father knows a lot of Apache. He gives them money, guns, whiskey.'

'What are you saying?' Hector asked.

'They could track us up here,' Sam said. 'They can track anything.'

'They can only track someone if they know where to start. There's no one coming, Sam.'

'But if—'

'If they do they still have to get by me.'

Sam was quiet for a moment. Then he said, 'You'd die for me?'

'I'd die for my job.'

Earlier that evening Ben and Hector had unlocked Sam from his cage and had smuggled him quietly out of the sheriff's office. They'd made him lie down in the back of a wagon, covered him with a tarp, and then they had slowly driven him out of town. About two miles out, amongst the trees on the lower slopes, two horses were saddled up and waiting. Hector had then taken Sam Cotton high up into the hills, and into the cave. He'd told the boy he wouldn't tie him up, but he'd better not try to escape. Sam had asked why all the sneaking about. Hector had told him that there was a lynch mob coming that night. 'How do you know?' Sam had asked. Hector had simply said, 'We know.' And later they'd heard the distant echoes of those gunshots.

'I'll probably be the one to die,' Sam said now. 'Once the judge arrives, I mean.'

'You tell him the truth, that's all you can do.'

'And if I can't?'

'If you can't tell the truth?' Hector said.

'Yes.'

'Why would you not tell the truth? You still trying to protect the girl?'

'Maybe.'

Sam saw Hector turn and look out across the great plain once again. After a long time Hector said, 'It's your choice, Sam. If you can't tell the truth then you'll probably die.'

*

In the darkness, lit only by the low moon and the spluttering remains of the gang's fire, Jim Cotton watched in horror as Amelia pulled the knife from the chest of the first man and lunged across to a second man, raising the knife to stab him too. Jim Cotton saw that across the camp one of the other men, now free from his blanket, was raising a gun.

The revolver he'd taken from the kid called Sam was in Jim's hand. He couldn't recall pulling it from his trousers but it was there and he couldn't let them kill Amelia. That would be as good as killing Sam.

He pulled the trigger and the man across the camp was blown back several feet and hit the ground.

He was vaguely aware of Amelia stabbing the second man, both of them screaming, but now another man was rising up, a rifle in his hand. Jim Cotton shot him. It took two bullets before the man went down.

Behind him, in the darkness, Jim Cotton could hear someone yelling. He could hear horses crying and whinnying, the sound of someone's footsteps on loose stones, of somebody rushing through undergrowth. The smell of cordite hung in the air and a cloud of smoke wreathed his hand and rose up towards his face.

Everything appeared to be happening slowly. The man Amelia was trying to kill rolled away from her, and she was attempting to stay with him, trying to stab him again and again, a crazed shriek coming from her lips. A man stood up across the camp and was aiming his pistol at Amelia.

The outlawed fired three times in quick succession.

Jim Cotton heard Amelia cry out – a different cry to her mad killing shriek – and she stumbled a few steps into the darkness and fell over.

The man who shot Amelia then turned his gun on Jim Cotton.

Jim was a split second ahead of him. If the man had used only two bullets on Amelia, Jim thought later, then he too would have been dead. But that third shot had given Jim just enough time to aim and fire, flames spitting out from the barrel of the gun, and now that man went down, his face, illuminated by moonlight, screwed up in agony.

Through ringing ears Jim Cotton could hear one man moaning and he could hear Amelia crying and gasping for air. Her breathing sounded liquid and hard. All the sounds were muffled and distant. He could taste the cordite now. He could smell gunpowder smoke, and he could feel every nerve ending burning on the surface of his skin.

His heart hammered and he felt pain in his arms and his head and in his belly. For a moment he thought that he was going to die. The gun was suddenly heavy in his hand. He felt sick.

'What the hell. . . ?' Someone called.

The guard.

Jim needed to go to Amelia. He *had* to go to Amelia. She was all that mattered. Everything, the hunger, the cold, the pain – the killing – was about Amelia. Without her he had nothing.

But there was still one more outlaw. *At least one more.* Jim tried to count those that he had killed, that Amelia had stabbed. But his head was too full of noise – the echoes of those deadly gunshots – and the memory of muzzle flashes that blinded him and made thinking almost impossible.

He found himself stepping back into the darkness beyond the perimeter of the camp just as the guard raced into the opening.

The man turned, looking this way and that in the darkness. He leaned over one man, then another. He crouched beside the one that was still breathing, still moaning.

'Charlie? Charlie, what in the hell happened?'

The one called Charlie tried to speak. It sounded to Jim like nothing more than the bubbling of spit and blood and air.

'Say again?'

'The . . . girl.'

The guard stood up and took two steps to where Amelia lay.

Jim suddenly realized that she wasn't making any sounds any more.

The guard prodded her with his foot.

'You bitch,' he said, and pointed his gun at her. 'Why in the hell you have to kill 'em all?'

'Because you all raped her,' Jim said, coming from the darkness, and pressing the hot barrel of his gun against the back of the guard's neck.

Even in the darkness the scene was like something from purgatory. The air smelled of blood and gunpowder and of bodily fluids and death. A complete silence had fallen over the surrounding area – no whisper of wind, or chatter of cicadas. It was as if nature herself had gone into shock over what had just happened.

Jim was fighting against shock, too. Not the shock over

what he had just done – although he knew he overstepped some mark that he had long imagined only other men, bad men, *terrible* men, ever came close to, let alone crossed – and he knew later that he would pay for what he'd done, both emotionally, physically, and in the eyes of God. But for now, he was able to block it all out. Jim was fighting against the shock of understanding, of comprehension.

If Amelia was dead, nothing else mattered. Everything had been in vain. There would be no one left to save Sam.

'Throw down the gun,' Jim said to the outlaw, who had been on guard duty when the slaughter had occurred.

The man didn't move. Jim could hear him breathing, the air rasping in the man's throat. He could sense tenseness in the man as if he was preparing to move suddenly.

Jim said, 'I'm about half an ounce of pressure away from blowing the bones right out of your neck. It would be a lot easier all round for me to do that.'

Still the man didn't move, he was wound up as tight as a violin string. Jim could smell the stench of whiskey on the man.

'You're right,' Jim said, and very quickly moved the gun two inches to the left, before pulling the trigger. The explosion was right beside the man's ear. Before the echo had even begun Jim pressed the smoking barrel against the man's neck again. The man flinched and Jim smelled burning flesh.

Now the man threw down his gun and it was only after he'd done so that Jim wondered how many bullets were left in the gun that he held. A good gunfighter would have known: Jim wasn't sure.

Jim turned the gun around in his hand, feeling the hot

barrel burning his own skin, and swiftly hit the man hard just above the right ear with the butt. Air exploded out of the man's lungs and he went down.

Jim picked up one of the lengths of rope that had been used to tie up Amelia. This length had been round her neck. It was already tied in a noose.

He quickly pass the loop of rope over the man's feet then hauled the rope tight as hard and fast as he could. Jim pulled the man's arms behind his back and tied the other end of the rope around his wrists. The man was already beginning to come round, moaning and coughing.

Jim checked his knots one final time and then rushed over to Amelia.

She was dead.

In the moonlight Tessa Brown watched Sheriff Benito Garcia take control of the town. He was like a good horseman rounding up cattle. Man by man he approached and spoke to the riders who had come into town to lynch Sam Cotton, and man by man they gave up their violence and started to drift back to the centre of town. Eventually, after a longer conversation than he'd had with any other individual he persuaded Skunk McLean to take his men and leave.

'I don't understand it,' Tessa said to Mort Mortensen. Mortensen was, out of everybody in Hope, the one man who knew everything. He had been a newspaper man in Philadelphia, or so he said, and the rumour was that he was looking to start something similar here in the territory. But Tessa secretly believed that such ambitions were no more than dreams. Mortensen was worn out. He had travelled long and hard uncovering and writing stories to send back home. He could – and for the price of drink often did – recount tales of Indians and buffalo hunters and gunfighters and mountain men, of wagon trains and railroad trains, of winter storms and cannibalism, stagecoach crashes, riverboats, sea-boats, captains and presidents. But now he rarely ventured beyond Pigeon Parker's livery. He walked with a limp, and always looked too thin. But he still had the journalist's knack of getting people to open up and tell him things. So Tessa had purposely gravitated towards him amongst all the groups of people on the street watching the show.

'You don't understand how he does it?' Mortensen said. 'Easy. He's a good sheriff. A hard man. Fearless, too. And everyone round these parts knows he's good with a gun.'

'I don't mean that,' Tessa said.

'He don't say much,' Mortensen went on. 'But when he does speak folks listen. Well, most of 'em most of the time. Sometimes a man just got to shoot his gun. And most folks know they'll come off second best with Ben.'

'I don't mean Sheriff Garcia doing this' – she swept her hand in the general direction of the retreating McLean gang – 'I mean, why do they want him – Sam – dead so badly? It was something Sheriff Garcia said in his office. He must be wondering on it, too.'

'Ahhh.'

'Ahhh?' she repeated.

'Ahhh, that would be a mystery,' Mortensen said. 'And it's something that I've pondered on, too.'

'It is?'

'Yesterday I could understand the way people reacted. Blood was running hot. Three good people had died and another is maybe on the way. But tonight? Why is Skunk McLean so keen to kill the boy before the judge gives him time to say his piece?'

'And?' She felt like she was about to learn something of great importance.

Mort Mortensen looked at her.

'I really don't know,' he said.

Jim Cotton wasn't aware of what he was doing. Grief and desperation flowed out of him as physically real as the sweat during the ride the previous day. He moaned and cried. He kicked at the bodies of the outlaws as he walked around the camp, his fists tight, tears on his cheeks. In the darkness horses whinnied. The man called Charlie wailed and in between his cries each liquid breath sounded as if it would be his last. The one Jim had hog-tied kept calling out asking what he intended to do.

At some point Jim Cotton looked down at the gun he held in his hand and realized it was empty save for one bullet.

He knelt down by one of the outlaws' bodies and started pulling bullets from the man's belt.

'What you gonna do,' the hogtied man said.

'What's your name?' Jim Cotton asked.

'Dalton. But I didn't do nothing.'

'You didn't do nothing?'

'The girl, I mean. I never touched her.'

The man called Dalton had twisted around on to his side, the moonlight illuminated his stubbled and dirty face. He grimaced in pain as Jim Cotton crouched beside him and pressed the barrel of his reloaded gun against the man's neck.

'I heard you,' Jim said.

'I didn't do nothing.'

'I heard you tell the kid back there she was ready for another go.' Jim Cotton spat on the ground.

'No. I didn't.'

'She's dead. You as good as killed her.'

The man's eyes were wide and frightened.

'I couldn't do it. Whiskey, you know?'

The man did indeed stink of whiskey. Whiskey and fear. Jim Cotton reached across and ratcheted back the hammer on the Colt.

'Please . . .' Dalton begged. 'I swear I never touched her.'

In the darkness the one called Charlie moaned, a long quiet moan that reverberated with gut-pain. 'Kill me,' he whispered. 'You got an itch to kill someone else, then kill me.'

'You're dying anyway,' Jim Cotton said without turning. 'It would be a waste of a bullet.'

Dalton said, 'Charlie's in agony, can't you hear?'

'*I* did it,' Charlie said. 'All of it. I poked the girl. I killed those folks back at the stage. I robbed that shop in Hope. God's sake . . . have mercy.' He started coughing, and the coughing became liquid and guttural and within seconds it metamorphosized into a long moan of agony.

Jim Cotton turned and looked towards the dying man.

'What did you say?'

Charlie said nothing.

91

'He said he's the one you should kill,' Dalton said. 'He's begging you.'

Jim Cotton took several steps across the darkness and now he knelt beside Charlie. The man was still breathing, but only just.

'What did you just say?' Jim Cotton was almost shouting. He had to hold himself back from shaking the man.

'Kill him,' Dalton said. 'Then kill me if you must. But for God's sake put Charlie out of his misery.'

'Nobody else is dying,' Jim Cotton said. 'Nobody at all.'

CHAPTER TEN

That night Hope never slept.

French John, a barman at the Domino, kept serving and people kept drinking and talking. Folks were back on the plank-walks, and they were standing by each other's front doors. They whispered about what had happened that night, and of what had happened the day before and the day before that – the shooting and the first attempted lynching – and they imagined what might happen come the morrow.

High in the hills, at the entrance to the cave in which they hid, Samuel Cotton and Hector Lopez sat quietly, wrapped in blankets, and watched the sky lighten. One by one the stars faded and disappeared and Sam wondered again on his mother's tale of the stars and if he himself would soon be one more bright light up there.

Hector Lopez blinked gritty tiredness from his eyes. He had to take Sam back into town shortly. Once the kid was back in his cell maybe he could catch an hour or two's sleep before it would start all again. He wasn't sure what time the judge was expected, or what the man would want to do – for all Hector knew the judge would want to bath, eat, maybe have a drink or several to relax after his stage-ride. Hell, a long stagecoach ride could take days to recover from. It might be a while yet before he would be able to hand Samuel over to justice. He hoped, though, with the judge in town, any attempts to pervert, anticipate, or accelerate the course of justice would be over.

Henry Herbert stood on the steps outside his hotel's porch in Black's Junction and breathed in the cool dawn air. It was his favourite time of day. Not too hot, no time yet for any troubles to have risen. And it was quiet. Henry chuckled to himself – it was always quiet out here. He'd lived places where there were always people shouting, music playing, dogs barking, and sellers selling. He could recall the incessant clang of metal on metal and the chink of glass on glass and the sound of water splashing against a wharf, bells and whistles, steam engines and hooters. Out here, save for the gentle whisper of the wind, the occasional banging of a hammer, and maybe the long sigh of a too-warm dog, you had to make your own noise. He stretched and wistfully longed for the East.

As he eased out of his stretch – which was about the most exertion he would undertake all day – he saw in the distance, looking north, a stagecoach approaching slowly along the trail. He pulled his pocket watch from his vest pocket and flicked it open, absent-mindedly noted that the ticking of the watch was a sound that he was always there, a sound he could rely on so long as he remembered to wind the watch – which he did now.

The stagecoach was right on time.

He watched it get closer and he didn't move until it pulled up outside the relay station. The driver nodded to him, then jumped down from the seat to go and arrange a change of horses. The man riding shotgun stayed put for the moment, his eyes alert, even here in the relative safety of the relay station. One of the stagecoach doors opened and a big man – almost as big as me, Herbert thought – climbed out. The man looked tired and pale.

'Where can I get a drink?' he said. 'Water, alcohol, coffee, I care not. These damn stagecoaches suck up all the dust. Sometimes I think it would be better to walk. Or at least ride.'

'Follow me, sir,' Herbert said, looking back over his shoulder to see if there was anyone else in the stagecoach. There was – a tall and lean younger man, wearing a gun and a red vest. He nodded at Herbert but made no sign of wanting to follow the portly man inside the hotel. Instead Herbert saw him walking over towards the well.

Herbert led the other man into the cool interior of the hotel.

'You do a lot of travelling, sir?' he asked.

'Seems like it's all I do.' The man held out his hand. 'Wilkes is the name. Judge Wilkes.'

A mile outside of Hope, Sheriff Benito Garcia said, 'He didn't try to run for it then?'

Hector Lopez made to reply but Samuel Cotton got in first. 'I've not done anything wrong. Why should I run? Anyway, I'm not the running kind.'

Garcia nodded. 'You were no trouble, then?'

'No.'

Garcia looked at Lopez. 'No trouble at all, boss,' Lopez said. 'How about down here. We heard some shooting.' He nodded into the distance where the old buildings and new tents of Hope could be seen. Already a heat haze was causing the air to shimmer above the town.

'Only what we expected. Nothing to worry about. No one got killed.'

'What happened?' Sam said. They were in the shade of some trees, hidden from casual view.

'Lynch mob turned up again.'

Sam nodded.

'Is it safe again now?' Sam asked.

Sheriff Benito Garcia looked at Hector Lopez and said, 'It is for the two of us. If I had been you I think I might have tried to run last night.'

Early afternoon, Joey, the ticket clerk from the Black's Junction relay stage, burst into Henry Herbert's hotel. Henry was sitting at one of the tables looking at a row of numbers in a heavy black book.

'Sir,' Joey said.

'Don't interrupt me, Joey,' Henry said. 'I think I've almost found the error. We may be a dollar or two richer than we thought.'

'Sorry, sir. But—'

'Joey!'

'Outside, sir. I think you should see this.'

Henry sighed. Joey was a good kid, a good clerk, but when he got to worrying something he was like a scratching dog. Henry shut the ledger. It was a quiet day, he'd have plenty of time to work the numbers again later.

'Outside,' Joey said again.

Henry stood up. One of his knee joints popped and his back ached. He wondered if that judge fellow who'd passed through earlier had the same problems on account of *his* weight. Henry followed Joey across the floorboards, noting that they needed sweeping to get rid of yet another layer of sand and dirt, and he walked out into the blinding sun. He squinted and narrowed his eyes and waited for his vision to clear.

There was a stagecoach stopped outside the hotel. An unscheduled coach, no less. The man up on the driving board didn't look as though he'd moved since hauling the coach to a stop. He still held the lines and he was still facing forward, but his head was slumped as if he was asleep. Behind the stagecoach there were a whole line of horses strung together. On the first one was a man sitting upright, his hands lashed together and then tied to the pommel. The man was breathing hard, his mouth open, his lungs gasping for air as if he'd been running. His face was thick with dust that he hadn't been able to wipe off with his tied hands. On each of the next three horses a body was tied face down over the saddle.

Henry Herbert took a step forward and then heard a low moaning coming from within the stagecoach. He rushed – as much as he ever rushed – forward and pulled open the stagecoach door.

He stepped back in horror, caught his own ankle, and fell backwards on to his generous behind.

Within a few seconds Joey was at his side, helping him up, sneaking a look inside the stagecoach.

The moaning was coming from a young man laid on the rear seat of the stagecoach. His face was white with blood loss and pain. His clothes were dirty and blood-soaked. The smell inside the stagecoach was like that of a slaughterhouse. Scores of flies were buzzing around.

On the front seat was a girl. Her clothes were equally as blood-soaked but her face was peaceful and calm. Flies crawled over her dress and her skin. She was clearly dead.

Herbert stepped backwards again, gasping for clean air. He was aware of men appearing from the other buildings and the tents, a small crowd gathering.

'My God,' he said. 'It's a moving charnel house.'

'Stagecoach from Hell,' Joey said.

Now the man up on the driving board raised his head and it took several seconds before Henry Herbert realized it was the fellow from the day before. What had he said his name was? Jim Cotton? The man looked in almost as bad shape as the fellow tied to the horse behind the stagecoach. His eyes were sunk deep into his face. Those eyes were ringed with black shadows and full of blood. His face and beard were thick with dirt and his lips were cracked and bleeding.

'Henry,' the man said. His voice was full of exhaustion and resignation.

'My God,' Henry Herbert said again. 'What happened?'

'The man in the back, the one on the horse needs water,' Jim Cotton said. 'So do the horses. Then me.' He stared into Henry Herbert's eyes and Henry saw pain and regret and horror in the man's gaze. 'The girl's dead,' Jim Cotton said, as if Henry mightn't have realized. 'The horses waited right by the coach,' he said, and added, 'The violin's broken.'

Then he slumped forward again.

The Junction men helped water and feed the horses, the prisoner, and the dying man. They retied knots and they refused the prisoner's – who said his name was Dalton –

pleas to free him. He swore he was innocent, that the one called Cotton had murdered them all. They tried to comfort the dying boy as much as they could, but there was little they could do for him. In one moment of lucidness he begged that someone shoot him. They refused.

In the hotel Jim Cotton sat at a table in the lobby, his hair and face damp, and his third jug of cool well-water half empty in front of him. He said to the crowd of men jostling to hear his story that the three dead men on horses were good men, passengers on a previous stage, and that they deserved a proper Christian burial and that's why he was taking them back to Hope. He said that there were half a dozen more men – the ones who had robbed the stagecoach and killed those three men – lying dead out there someplace.

'I left them to the buzzards.'

'You killed 'em all?' someone asked.

'I had to.'

'The one in the back of the stagecoach is the one. . . .' He looked at Henry Herbert. 'Do you recognize him?'

'I don't know. I didn't look closely enough.'

'Go and look.'

'Now?'

'Now.'

A minute later Henry came back in having opened the door on the charnel house stagecoach once again.

'Well?' Jim Cotton said.

'I'm not sure. I guess it could be the boy who was here a few days ago.'

'The one who was agitated?' Jim Cotton asked.

'Yes.'

'It is him,' Jim Cotton said. 'He's the one robbed the mercantile back in Hope and killed Jackson, Queenie, and Ima. He admitted it. I'm praying he stays alive long enough for them to hang him.'

As if struck by something, Jim Cotton suddenly looked up, the fastest movement any of them had seen him make since he had rolled death-like into the junction. 'Has the judge been through?' he asked.

'This morning,' Henry said. 'Not long after dawn. Right on time.'

Pain flickered across Cotton's face. 'We need to go,' he said. 'We need to hurry.'

'We?' Henry Herbert said.

'You're coming with me. You're a witness that that boy was in here spending Irwin Foote's silver dollars and being all agitated too.'

'I'm needed here.'

'The prisoner – Dalton – he's going to testify, too. Between us all we can save my boy.'

'I don't know. I'm—'

Jim Cotton reached down to his pants belt and pulled out the .45 with which he'd done more killing in the last night than most men do in a lifetime. He put the gun on the table. A couple of the men breathed out audibly. It was one thing to shoot rabbits and even to brag about shooting men, but here was a gun that had dealt out more death in the last few hours than any of them would dare boast of outside of their fantasies.

'I ain't asking,' he said. 'You can ride shotgun or you can sit inside with the boy and the girl. But you're coming, Henry.'

CHAPTER ELEVEN

There was a note tacked on to the schoolhouse door saying *No Lessons Today*. Mort Mortensen knocked on the door. It was late afternoon. When Tessa Brown opened the door he couldn't help but raise his eyebrows at how fine she looked.

She noticed his expression and said, 'The word is that the judge wants to hold the court at five. He says he doesn't like to waste time. Unofficially the word is that he likes to get business out of the way so he can enjoy a drink, and maybe something else in the saloon, before leaving tomorrow.'

Mortensen nodded, he'd heard the same. The judge had told Garcia that if anyone wanted to think bad of him for relaxing after a session then that was their lookout.

'Sentencing a man to death is not an easy thing to carry around with you,' Judge Wilkes had told the sheriff. 'I don't think anyone would begrudge me a whiskey afterwards.'

Garcia had apparently said, 'You already know the outcome?'

Wilkes had told him not to be smart, that he was talking figuratively.

'Just so long as everyone gets a fair trial,' Garcia said.

To which the judge had replied, 'We have a horse thief and a triple murderer, I believe. Have no fear, both will get a fair trial.'

Now Tessa said to Mortensen, 'It only seemed right to wear my Sundays. For Samuel.'

'You think he's going to be found—?'

'The whole town is against him, Mort. What chance has he got? If I can put in a good word for him I will. Someone must.'

'What about Jim?'

She shook her head. 'He went after the McLean girl I believe. But . . . I don't know. He's not here.'

'That doesn't sound like Jim.'

'I know. I'm worried to death.'

'Are you . . . you and him. . . ?' She could see something in his eyes, the same something that had been there when she'd opened the door and he'd first seen her with her hair up and her best clothes on.

'I don't know,' she said. 'I don't think so. Jim Cotton . . . his wife . . . it was a long time ago but I don't think he's ever got over it.' Their eyes met. 'Anyway, what about you? What brings you knocking on my door?'

'About what we were talking around last night. I've been asking questions. Trying to find out what I can.'

'And?'

He shook his head.

'You haven't found anything out?'

'I haven't found anything out about why McLean is so

102

keen to see Sam Cotton dead. Not aside from a family feud that goes back a generation anyway.'

'Oh.'

'But. . . .'

'Mort Mortensen,' she said, 'whatever it is, will you please spit it out?'

'OK, OK. If you speak to the right people and put their stories together it would seem that there's no longer any silver in Skunk McLean's mine. It's worked out, Tessa. Empty.'

She looked at him and tried to determine if this was good news, bad news, or simply irrelevant news.

'I don't get it,' she said. 'I don't understand the connection.'

'Me neither. But—'

'But what?'

'There must be some significance.'

'There *might* be some significance.'

'Exactly,' he said, excitedly.

'Mort,' she said, looking around at the clock on the classroom wall. 'In thirty minutes Judge Wilkes is starting the trials. What are you going to find out in thirty minutes?'

He looked deflated.

'I just thought it might be of interest.'

She reached out and touched his hand. 'Thank you, Mort. It is of interest. But I'm not sure it's enough to save Sam's life.'

The trial was to be held in the room used as the town hall. When not being used for town meetings the room served as a storage area for both dirty and clean linen, cleaning materials, tools, and food. It served as an eating room and a sleeping room for hotel staff, an office and, for a while, a place to isolate a dozen healthy pigs when swine fever crept through the town the previous year. There was no roof – the room had been covered with a canvas tarpaulin for almost a year. Extra chairs for spectators were brought across from the saloon and folks were queuing for a place from mid afternoon onwards.

Skunk McLean and a large group of hands rode into town about an hour before proceedings were due to start. They hitched their horses outside the Domino saloon. McLean told his men that he had a little business to attend to over at the sheriff's office and to line up a few whiskies for him. He'd only be a few minutes.

It took him ten, but when he came back into the saloon he was smiling. 'It's going to be a fine trial,' he said to his men, and downed two shots before saying, 'You all know what you got to do? You know your stations?'

They nodded as one.

'You got the rope?'

'Yep.'

'Good. You wait for my signal.'

He looked at French John behind the bar.

'I heard the judge is in town.'

'Yes.' There was no accent in French John's speech. His grandfather had been born in Paris, his father in New York, and he in Philadelphia. His surname was Lafayette but he'd not used it since stepping west of the Mississippi.

'About time.'

French John refilled all the shots.

'Jury picked and ready to go?' McLean said.

'So I understand.'

McLean twisted around. 'Any of them in here?'

'No, sir. From what I understand they were only chosen this afternoon and the judge has them over in the hotel.'

'Doesn't want anyone to . . . have a quiet word in their ears, huh?'

'I couldn't say.'

'How about the prosecution?'

'I don't know.'

'Defence? Who should I be aiming my vitriol at? I'd like a word with anyone who's prepared to defend that kid. He's as guilty as sin and we could all have saved ourselves a lot of trouble if folks had listened to me.'

'I don't know who's defending the boy, sir.'

'You don't know much, do you?'

'Another drink, sir?'

Skunk McLean smiled. 'I think I just might.'

By fifteen of five a dozen men had scrambled on to the walls of the town hall room and had rolled back the canvas roof to give themselves a bird's eye view of proceedings. Inside, the area reserved for spectators was already packed. The jurors were led in by Hector Lopez and they sat on chairs that had been laid out in two rows on the right hand side of the room. Lopez stood against the wall behind them cradling a shotgun and watching the door and, occasionally, the open roof.

In the hotel lobby, Tessa Brown was insisting that Rube Rubin – the man whose name had been drawn out of the hat earlier that day to defend both Samuel Cotton and the horse-thief Floyd Casey – call her as a witness.

'There's no one else,' she said. 'I know the boy. I know he wouldn't have done this. Let me at least speak on his behalf.'

Rubin had passed the bar in Chicago and had figured to make a name for himself out West. Turned out a lot of other lawyers felt the same. There had been nine names in the hat. His friend, colleague, and also a Chicagoan, Stefan Schwam, had picked up the prosecution. They'd had a couple of shots together at the Domino earlier and had agreed that it was already in the bag for Schwam – both cases, horse-thief and murderer.

Rubin said, 'His father's still not turned up?'

'No,' Tessa Brown replied.

Rubin sighed. There was little enough hope for the kid as it was. It didn't help that the father had run off. 'OK,' he said. 'You might be all I've got. But you know. . . .'

'What?'

'It feels like the whole town is against him. Are you sure you want to stand up for him?'

'Someone has to. He's a good boy.'

'If you're absolutely sure.'

'I'm sure,' she lied. 'Is it. . . ? Sam's trial, is it first or second? I mean, Floyd Casey is up, too, isn't he?'

'There's a funny thing,' Rubin said. 'I was to defend Floyd too, but a few minutes ago – just before you arrived, in fact – I had word that the charges against Floyd had been dropped. A misunderstanding apparently.'

'Oh,' she said, thinking why couldn't the charges against Sam be dropped as well. That surely was also a misunderstanding.

106

Rube Rubin pulled a silver railroad watch from his vest pocket.

'We'd better go,' he said. 'It's time.'

Skunk McLean and his two henchmen pushed their way into the crowd filling every available inch at the spectators' end of the room. Already the seats had been edged forward three or four feet and were starting to encroach on the jurors' space and on the area where Rube and Stefan would stand to make their pitches. The accused would be standing, Benito Garcia had told Hector Lopez, cuffed and guarded by Benito over by the far door.

The body heat of all the men – and a couple of women – was already clouding the atmosphere in the room. Lopez silently thanked the initiative of the spectators who had climbed up on to the roof and had rolled back the canvas. At least that let some of the heat – and body smell – out, even though it also let the last of the late sun in.

'There's no room left,' someone said to McLean. 'You're too late. You should've queued up like the rest of us.'

McLean, dressed in his brown corduroy and appearing more barrel-chested than ever, looked the man in the eye, his stare not wavering. After several seconds the man squeezed himself backwards to let McLean by.

In the front row of the spectators' seats three of McLean's hands who had arrived in town earlier stood up and let McLean and his two men take over their seats.

Hector Lopez watched and waited and eventually Skunk's gaze landed on the deputy. Hector held the man's gaze and at the same time slowly let the shotgun drop a few inches. His message, he hoped, was clear. Behave. Or else.

*

Rube Rubin directed Tessa Brown towards a spare chair over where the witnesses were sitting. Raoul Vega and Martha Kane were already seated there, as were a couple of cowboys whom Tessa recognized from around town but wasn't sure who they were. Maybe they'd been the guys who'd cornered Sam up on the north trail a few days back.

Raoul and Martha and the cowboys nodded, but in all their eyes was a look of accusation, a look of puzzlement that someone was here to possibly speak on behalf of the killer.

When she looked around the room she saw Skunk McLean, his face red, his eyes angry, staring at her. She tried to stare back but was only able to maintain the connection for a few seconds.

The noise in the room was incredible, even with the roof off. People were talking and shouting, laughing and coughing. Chair legs scraped on the wooden floor and a corner of the rolled back canvas roof slapped and banged in the slight wind.

Tessa took a deep breath, trying to calm herself. She heard a door opening, saw Skunk McLean standing, and the noise suddenly reached even greater volumes.

'Killer!' someone yelled. 'There's the bastard! We should hang him now!'

She looked round.

Sam Cotton was led into the corner of the room nearest the door by Benito Garcia. Sam's head was down, his shoulders slumped.

He looked tired and scared, she thought.

He looked resigned to dying.

CHAPTER TWELVE

Stefan Schwam, the prosecutor, said to Martha Kane, 'You were there when it happened?'

'I was outside.'

'Did you see the attacker's face?'

'No. I mean, yes.' Martha looked older than she had a few days before. Tired, too. There were new lines on her face, Tessa thought. And Stefan was giving her quite a grilling as if it had been she who had done the shooting in the mercantile a few days back.

'No, you mean yes?' he repeated. 'You saw him, or you saw his face?'

'I *think* I saw his face,' she said. 'It's all a blur.' Martha Kane couldn't bring herself to look at Sam Cotton, standing over there by the door into the hotel, his hands in chains, the sheriff holding one of his arms just above the elbow. Now and again Sam would look up, glance around the room, look back at the door, but even when his eyes met Tessa's she didn't think he was seeing her. He probably didn't even know that she was on his side. All the witnesses so far had been against him.

'And did you recognize him?'

'No.' There was a rumble of puzzlement from the spectators.

'No?'

'I mean, not then. I didn't really see him. I was talking to . . . I don't remember. The first thing I knew was when I heard gunshots. Then screaming.' Now she did glance over at Sam. He caught her eyes and shook his head slowly. She snapped her gaze away. 'It all happened so quickly.'

'Did you see the attacker go into the store?' Schwam said.

'No.'

'But you saw him come out.'

'He had his hat pulled down. He was running. Fast.'

'But you recognized him.'

'I'd heard shots. I knew Jackson. . . .'

Tessa saw tears rolling down Martha Kane's cheeks.

'It's all right, Mrs Kane, please take your time.'

She dabbed the tears away with a tiny white handkerchief. Someone at the spectators' end of the room said '*bastard*' and there was a murmour of agreement. A tomato – launched from unseen hands – hit Sam Cotton on the shoulder. It plopped to the floor looking like a chunk of bloody flesh. Several people laughed.

A shot rang out.

Men ducked, a few tried to pull guns from holsters but the crowd was so pressed together that most found it impossible.

A second shot rang out and Tessa – and most of the people in the room – realized it was Judge Wilkes smashing his hammer down on the table behind which he sat.

'Decorum!' he shouted. Then he looked round and, as if a little unsure whom to report it to, said to Sheriff

Garcia, 'Sorry, but I put a split in your table. Don't know my own strength.'

Behind the judge, the younger man in the red vest who had arrived on the same stagecoach as Wilkes stood motionless, eyes scanning the room.

'May we go on?' Schwam said.

'You may.'

'The attacker had shot your husband, Mrs Kane. Then came running out. What happened then?' Schwam asked.

Martha Kane said, 'I don't know. I'm sorry. It was . . . it was chaotic. The next thing I can remember is being in there with Jackson. There was blood . . . so much blood.'

Someone shouted out once more and again Judge Wilkes had to hammer on the table. 'If I have to do that again I'm doing it on someone's head,' he said. Then, to Martha Kane, 'Carry on.'

'They were all dead,' she said quietly. 'There was so much blood.'

'What was the attacker wearing, Mrs Kane?' Schwam asked.

'What was he wearing?'

'Yes.'

She looked briefly again at Sam. 'He was wearing what he's wearing now.'

'You're sure?'

'When they brought him in I had no doubts,' she said.

'But you have doubts now?'

One more glance at the young man. He was staring at the floor.

'No,' she said. 'I have no doubts.'

*

Judge Wilkes – and the jury – heard from several of the cowboys who had been riding on the west trail trying to track down the killer. When they'd spotted Sam Cotton he'd ridden, they'd all agreed, like he'd had the Devil himself on his tail.

Rube Rubin, for the defence, stood up and said to the last of these cowboys, but really addressing his comments to the jury.

'It's conjecture, isn't it?'

'Sorry, sir?' the cowboy asked. He was holding his hat in front of him like a shield, clearly nervous to be standing in front of judge and jury if only as a witness. Tessa Brown watched as he spun the hat round and round in his hands. They hadn't got to the defence witnesses yet and her own nerves were growing. The feeling in the room, an ongoing hum of whispers and comments and spitting and cursing, was growing against Sam and she couldn't help but wonder what it would mean for her when she stood up to defend him. She had no illusions that life in Hope was going to be awkward afterwards. Maybe even impossible.

It was a thought that scared her enough to make her think of running from the room – something she may well have done had not the door to the street been impossible to access because of the crush of spectators.

'Conjecture,' Rubin said. 'There could have been a hundred reasons why Sam Cotton was riding up there. And he could have simply been scared when he saw a group of men chasing him down. No wonder he ran, figuratively speaking.'

'Name me one,' the cowboy said.

'One?'

'You said there could have been a hundred reasons. Name me one, sir.' There was a ripple of laughter from the spectators.

'It's my job to ask the questions,' Rubin said. 'And it's also my job to point out that all the evidence is circumstantial.' He turned to face the jury. 'Martha Kane – who, understandably wants to see someone punished for the terrible murder of her husband – never even saw the attacker's face. She says she's not mistaken about the clothes he was wearing – but she saw Sam Cotton dragged back into town, she's seen him with a noose around his throat, and she's seen him in this courtroom today, all in the same clothes. I suggest that it would be very easy for her to be mistaken about clothes on account of she's believing what she *thinks*, not what she *knows*.'

'Objection,' Stefan Schwam said. 'He's casting aspersions on my witness's memory.'

'Aspersions,' the judge repeated.

'Yes sir, aspersions.'

'Objection upheld.'

'You can't possibly hang a man based on the so-called evidence set out this afternoon,' Rubin said. 'I know emotions are running high, but there is no *actual* evidence.'

'I'll be the judge of what we're going to do with the boy,' Wilkes said. He looked at Stefan Schwam. 'Any more prosecution witnesses? We need to move things along faster than we are.'

Stefan Schwam said, 'Just one more witness, Your Honour.' He looked at Rube Rubin, tilted his head very slightly as if apologizing, and said, 'In terms of evidence, how does a confession grab you?'

113

Then he turned to the door and nodded. Someone reached out and opened the door and Floyd Casey, the horse thief, squeezed in.

Floyd took the oath, then Schwam said, 'You've something to tell us, I believe, Mr Casey.'

Floyd Casey looked at the judge, then at Schwam and finally at Sam Cotton.

'We were in the cages next to each other,' he said. 'After they tried to hang him the first time and he was put back inside he said to me . . . he was scared, you understand, but he said to me. . . .'

Sam was shaking his head and muttering *no no no*. Noise was growing from the spectators over to Tessa's left. Someone on the roof shouted *bastard* again and the judge had to crack the table once more. Tessa felt the rooms start to spin slightly. The word *misunderstanding* kept bouncing around her head.

'He told me he did it,' Floyd Casey said. 'He told me it was he who killed them all.'

Tessa Brown said, 'He's a good boy.'

People jeered.

The prosecutor, Stefan Schwam said, 'That's it? That's all you have to offer? "He's a good boy".'

The room was too hot. The smell of people, of old sweat, of dirt ingrained into clothes, rose up and caused her throat to tighten as surely as if someone had their hand wrapped around her wind-pipe. Her vision blurred – she thought it might be tears. Her legs trembled and her hands shivered with nerves.

When Rube had turned to her he had whispered 'OK?'

and she had nodded, but now she wasn't at all sure. People had sworn and laughed and someone had thrown a tomato at her. The judge had cracked his hammer and then, when all faces and ears were upon her, she realized that she didn't really have anything to say. Nothing to compare with real witnesses and reports – genuine or not – of confessions.

'I've known him all his life,' she said, willing her voice to strong and steady. 'He's God-fearing. He wouldn't have done—'

'He had an itch in his pants!' someone cried out. 'That'll change a boy all right.'

More laughter.

'The Samuel Cotton that I know, that you all know' – she forced herself to look slowly around the room – 'wouldn't – and didn't – do this.'

'Comments noted,' Judge Wilkes said, rather indifferently. He looked across at Stefan Schwam. 'Any further questions from the prosecution?'

Schwam smiled, 'No, Your Honour. I don't think any more are needed.'

The jury were led out the inside door and taken to a room to make their deliberations. Judge Wilkes told them they had half an hour, but if they could take less time that would sit OK with him.

Nobody left the room. It was noisy and hot and smelling ever more thickly of sweat and farts and stale air. Tessa felt as if she'd taken a several punches. She wished she'd been stronger when she had been stood up – made her case better. But at least someone had defended Sam. She found herself staring at Skunk McLean. He was drinking from a silver flask and smiling broadly, joking with the men sat next to him.

She had been wondering who had put Floyd Casey up to it – she didn't believe for a moment that Sam had made the confession that Casey had testified about – and now, looking at how relaxed and happy McLean appeared she found the answer. Somebody had told her – maybe Mort Mortensen, maybe Jim Cotton, perhaps just something she'd picked up on the street – that it had been McLean's horses that Floyd Casey had been accused of stealing. Out of the blue those charges had been dropped and almost simultaneously Casey had appeared as a witness spouting forth that Sam had confessed to him.

But what could she do about it? It had been hard enough just to stand and say what she'd said let alone make any unsubstantiated accusations of her own.

The truth, Tessa realized, was that Sam – standing with his head down in the corner, fingers laced together as if in prayer – was being lynched in this room just as surely as he had almost been in the street just a few days before.

The jury took just fifteen minutes to consider their verdict.

They filed back in and Judge Wilkes had the juror nearest him stand up.

'You've reached a verdict,' he said. It wasn't a question. 'What is it?'

The man cast a swift look towards Sam. Tessa saw the sheriff grip Sam's arm harder. She couldn't help but think he was helping Sam stay upright rather than preventing him trying to run.

The man said, 'He's guilty, Your Honour.'

CHAPTER THIRTEEN

It was the sound of gunfire and hollering that woke Jim Cotton. He hadn't realized he was asleep. He had been awake when he'd turned the stagecoach on to the quiet main street of Hope, hardly registering the lack of people on the boardwalks. The low sun had been burning into his eyes all the way back from Black's Junction and much of the time he hadn't known what was real and what wasn't. Rocks and trees had become people – old soldier friends, his wife, his father, his mother. Alongside him on the board Henry Herbert had kept prodding him awake, telling him they were almost there. At some point a few miles back the moaning in the back of the stagecoach had ceased, but the one called Dalton – tied to the lead trailing horse – kept shouting, pleading his innocence, asking for water. At one point he'd called out that he'd tell the truth, tell what really happened if they would let him go.

It sounded like a battle was taking place just off the side of the hotel. Then Jim heard the hollering and cheering and laughing and in his awakening heart he knew what had just happened.

*

When the worst of the noise had died down Judge Wilkes banged on the table again and said, 'Make space, make space.'

'When are we going to hang him?' someone yelled.

'We still have the rope ready,' McLean called out and several people laughed and clapped hands. McLean smiled and said, almost to himself, 'I'm not joking.'

'Bring the prisoner forward,' Wilkes said.

Ben Garcia brought Sam into the middle of the room. Tessa saw that Sam's hands were shuddering. Even his shoulders were trembling.

'Samuel Cotton,' the judge said, 'You have been found guilty of the terrible murder of' – he glanced down at a piece of paper on the table – 'of Jackson Kane, Queenie Vega, and Ima Rodriquez. You have been found guilty by a jury of your peers in a fair trial.'

He looked at Sam.

'Son, this is an awful thing you've done. Three people for a few coins. Before I sentence you, do you have anything to say?'

Sam looked up. He swallowed.

'I didn't do it,' he said.

'Horse shit!' someone shouted, and people cheered.

'We've established that you did,' Wilkes said. 'I'm giving you an opportunity to say sorry for what it's worth. Maybe explain why.'

'I didn't do it,' Sam said again, his voice quiet.

'Just hang him!' someone yelled.

'You have nothing else to say?' Judge Wilkes asked Sam.

'I didn't do it.'

The judge nodded. 'Then I have no alternative to sentence you to be taken from this court room and hanged from the neck until you are dead. May God have mercy on your soul.'

There was more cheering and gunfire, louder than even when the verdict had been announced.

Tears rolled down Tessa's face. She looked up through the unfinished roof at the darkening sky trying to see God up there, trying to understand, but all she saw were the roof-top spectators cowering away from the bullets that were being fired skywards. Smoke, and now the smell of gunpowder and the sound of applause and cheering filled the room. She bowed her head and closed her eyes but immediately felt as if she was imagining things for the last thing she thought she had seen was someone pushing their way in, the spectators over by the door pressing back to give them room, a hush falling, and now she imagined she heard the judge saying, 'What is this? *Who* is this?'

Henry Herbert was uncomfortable with the gun. But he figured the fellow in front of him – the one called Dalton – didn't know that. Plus, Dalton was carrying the body of the kid who had died somewhere between Hope and Black's Junction. Dalton wasn't going to be making any quick moves.

And anyway, this was a tale he was going to be able to live off – and embellish – for the rest of his life. Nothing like this had ever happened back East.

'What is this? *Who* is this?' Judge Wilkes said. Henry recognized him from earlier that day.

119

Henry stepped out from behind Dalton so that the judge could see him clearly.

'Henry Herbert, Your Honour. We met earlier today at the hotel in Black's Junction.'

'Get him out of here!' McLean said, standing up at the opposite end of the room. 'There's a trial going on. Actually, the trial is over. We're about to hang someone.' McLean glanced briefly upwards as if looking for a signal. Or maybe giving a signal.

Henry looked across at the big man. There was something desperate in the man's voice, in his eyes. He had a riding crop in his hand, too. There was a sense of evilness coming off the man in waves – like a smell or a sound. Henry shuddered and felt sweat on the palms of his hand. Suddenly he didn't think he would be able to fire the gun even if he had to.

'Sit down,' Judge Wilkes said, banging his hammer on the splintered table.

'The trial is over,' McLean said. 'Verdict and sentencing. It's time to carry out—'

'Sit down!'

McLean glanced upwards again, then sat down and started whispering to the man next to him.

'Who is this?' the judge asked yet again, looking at Henry and then moving his gaze towards Dalton.

It was so noisy and hot in the room that Henry thought he'd never again long for the clang and clatter of the harbourside back East.

'The fellow standing up is called Dalton,' he said. 'The one's he's holding . . . the one's he's just dropped, is Charlie. I don't know Charlie's surname. I do know he's dead and I do know he's the one who robbed the mercantile here in Hope a few days back.'

There was an explosion of yelling and swearing, chairs were knocked over. McLean was on his feet again. The judge was banging on his table to no avail. Dalton glanced round at Henry with a look of fear in his eyes. Henry thought Dalton might be about to run so he held the gun a little higher.

'Tell the judge what Charlie told you,' he said. 'What Charlie told you and Jim.'

McLean was striding forward now, his face beet-red, his riding crop swishing in his hand.

'You're too late!' he said. 'Too late!'

The judge banged on the table again and yelled for quiet.

'It's true,' Dalton said, his voice husky with dust. 'Charlie was the one.' His voice was so quiet and croaky that only those closest to him heard.

'Everyone shut up!' Judge Wilkes yelled, struggling to hear. McLean snapped his riding crop down across Dalton's face opening up a long red weal. Dalton stepped backwards and collided with Henry Herbert. McLean pressed forwards after them but caught his foot on the body of Charlie. Henry, Dalton, and McLean all fell to the floor, McLean landing on the soft body of Charlie. A cloud of flies buzzed upwards.

People lunged forwards. One of McLean's men tried to help McLean up. Henry Herbert felt Dalton trying to take the gun away from him. He tried to pull it away from Dalton, terrified what would happen if the outlaw got hold of the gun.

121

There was the sound of a gunshot very close.

For a moment Henry had the terrible thought that he'd just shot someone. He looked at Dalton's dusty pale face. Dalton looked at him. There was no pain in the outlaw's face.

Then someone whispered 'Oh my God', and for a moment the crush eased. Henry could see the young man in the red vest now standing in front of the judge, a smoking gun held in his hand. The sheriff, still holding Sam Cotton, had moved him back against the far wall away from all the trouble.

But everyone was looking towards Henry, no, *beyond* Henry, at the door just behind him.

He turned and saw Jim Cotton standing there carrying the lifeless body of the girl.

Jim Cotton saw everything through a haze of exhaustion and heat stroke, dried blood and trail dirt. He walked into the room behind Henry Herbert and discovered chaos. The girl was no weight in his arms. In fact he couldn't feel his arms. He heard shouting and gunfire as if from a long way away and he saw McLean jumping to his feet and yelling at Henry and Dalton that they were too late. He saw panic and fear in McLean's eyes and he saw the man raise his crop and hit Dalton. He heard the judge yelling for calm and he heard McLean telling the judge that it was too late – the verdict was in. He saw Ben Garcia pulling Sam to safety across the far side of the room, over there by Tessa Brown and Martha Kane, and he locked eyes with Sam, saw the loneliness and fear in his son's eyes. Then people were falling over in front of him and a fellow he didn't know – a young gunslinger by the looks of it was drawing his gun and firing a warning shot.

And then he was aware that everyone was looking at him, clearly visible in the doorway now.

Amelia McLean dead in his arms.

Sam Cotton let out a long howl of anguish.

His world had narrowed to an ever diminishing band of light these last few days. Each hour seemingly bringing with it more darkness. Just when he thought the darkness had become as all encompassing as it ever could – sentenced to hang, all the townsfolks that he had once considered his friends cheering and laughing at him, Skunk McLean, whom Sam hated for what he had threatened to do to Amelia, smiling and nodding and shaking hands with his side-kicks, knowing that Sam's time was now numbered in hours, maybe only minutes – all this with the one tiny speck of white light which was that Amelia was still out there, still alive, still breathing, still part of this earth. At least there was that. There was always that.

Of course, there was his father, too. Another speck of light. Just to lock eyes with his father helped ease all that darkness. He'd wondered where his father had been this last day. He'd never doubted that his father would be here.

But everything good in the world – including his father's return – was negated by the terrible thing his father carried into the room. Sam had long ago given up hope on life, or hope that Amelia would be able to testify on his behalf. But at least she had been out there and free.

'No,' he said. 'Nooooo. . . .' The word rising from deep

within, getting louder, drawing every last good thing from this world and expelling it outwards, turning into a howl, a cry of pain and despair.

He fell to his knees, pulling Ben Garcia down with him, and he heard his anguished sob echo back to him.

It felt as if something burst within Skunk McLean's head. Somewhere just behind the eyes he felt a blinding pain. For a moment he wondered if one of those gunshots that had been randomly fired had ricocheted into his head. But he knew it wasn't that. It was a deeper pain as if something had reached down with a claw-like hand and had torn the very soul right out from within him.

It was Cotton's fault. It always was and it always would be. The evidence was there before them. That was why the boy needed to die. One reason anyway. There was another that he couldn't quite piece together right now. But it was the truth. And they'd just about been there. The joy at finally hearing the kid pronounced guilty – and not just that – but being sentenced to hang that very evening. Right there and then. It was righteous. It was how it was meant to be. Everyone would say he'd been correct all along and that they should have hanged Sam that first day. He had felt a glow come across him as if God himself had patted him on the back.

Then suddenly someone else had come into the room *after* the trial had finished. It should have been too late, but here they were – someone he didn't know carrying the body of a kid. Any kid. A *random* kid. Saying this is the one who did it. Was that the best that Jim Cotton could do? Find a kid who looked a bit like Sam, shoot the kid, rough him up, dress him in similar clothes and make out that he did it? It was so clearly nonsensical that McLean couldn't even comprehend why the judge was even listening. Yet that's what he'd been about to do. But McLean wasn't having that. No sir. The trial was over. The verdict was in. *It was too late.* The Cotton boy had been sentenced to die and that was that. He'd stood up to make that point – a valid point – and by the roars and cheers he knew he had the town with him, but the judge looked like he wanted to listen. Who did the judge think he was anyway? And somehow McLean had lost his temper, he'd whipped that man across the face – not sure who he was and then they'd fallen down and when he'd looked up there had been Jim Cotton and Jim Cotton had in his arms . . . and that was when the explosion had taken place behind his eyes.

It had been Amelia. It was Amelia. Jim Cotton had killed some random kid and now he had killed Amelia, and Skunk McLean roared like a lion and white light burned behind his eyes and he was upon Jim Cotton, trying to kill the man he hated so much, hands around Cotton's throat, tears pouring down his cheeks and Amelia's body on the floor beneath him. Every time he pressed harder at Cotton's throat he felt his own daughter's skin and bones and flesh below him. He roared again and squeezed harder, seeing Jim Cotton's eyes bulging and the weak old man not even putting up a fight.

Someone grabbed Tessa Brown's hand. For a moment she didn't know who it was. She couldn't take her eyes off the scene in front of her. Big Skunk McLean had his hands around Jim Cotton's throat and was squeezing the life out of him. He was smashing Jim's head on to the floor even as he tried to strangle him. All around people were yelling and across the room where the spectators had been sitting several people were grappling with each other.

Tessa glanced to her right and saw that it was Martha Kane who was gripping her hand. Martha's face was white. She had been through so much this last week and she looked terribly thin and frail. Despite the fact that Martha's testimony had helped put Sam where he was now Tessa still felt a pang of sorrow for the woman. She'd lost her husband. She'd seen him die. Held him as he'd died. And she was saying something now.

'What?' Tessa said. 'I can't hear.'

'It could've been him,' Martha Kane said.

Tessa looked back at the chaos in front of her. Hector Lopez had his arms around McLean's neck and was trying to haul him off Jim Cotton but the man was too heavy, his fury too large. One of McLean's cowboys was trying to pull Lopez off McLean.

Then, as if choreographed, she saw the young man in the red vest – the judge's bodyguard – step forward and Ben Garcia, too. The young man pressed his gun against McLean's cowboy's head and using the barrel pushed him away from McLean, and Ben Garcia turned his own gun backwards and rapped Skunk McLean behind the ear with the handle. Skunk turned for a moment, a puzzled expression on his face, and then he rolled over on to his side, unconscious.

Tessa could hear Jim Cotton gasping for air. Sam was over there by the door now, he was kneeling unsteadily between his father and Amelia McLean's body, not knowing where to look, to whom to go.

Another shot echoed out and now Judge Wilkes, a small gun smoking in his hand, yelled, 'Stop right there, Dalton.'

Tessa saw that the man who had first stepped through the door carrying the body of a young man had taken the opportunity of the mayhem to edge towards the door.

The one called Dalton stopped and put his hands in the air.

'It could have been him,' Martha Kane whispered. 'I don't know.'

Tessa looked at her again.

'Who?'

'The dead boy,' she said. 'He might have been the one. They all look so alike these days.'

Skunk McLean came out of his darkness his head hurting so much that he was convinced it really was cleaved in two. All he knew for certain was that they were trying to take justice away from him.

He was on all fours, his mouth full of blood. He spat on the floor and made it on to his knees. Then unsteadily to his feet. All around him the chaos was dying down. That damn judge, fat and old as he was, seemed to be taking control. He was ordering them all to sit, all those towns-folks, and they were doing as they were told, sitting down like sheep, if sheep ever sat down. Someone had placed a coat over Amelia's body, and a blanket over the other one – the one Jim Cotton had killed and was trying to pass off as the real killer.

Cotton – Jim Cotton – was over there sitting where the

127

witnesses had been. He was drinking from a jug of water that yet another fat man that McLean didn't know was holding to his lips. Next to Cotton, the one called Dalton was standing up, Hector Lopez next to him, shotgun still in his hand. Sam Cotton was there too, and the sheriff still had hold of his chains. That was good. At least the kid was still in chains.

McLean was aware of people looking at him as he made it, swaying, to his feet.

He looked down at the covered body of his daughter and felt grief course through him, enough grief to make him stumble and reach out for support. His hand found the back of a chair.

He raised his gaze and looked at the judge, at Jim Cotton, at the sheriff over there guarding the killer Sam Cotton. He let his eyes roll right over the new man who'd come in, and he scarcely noticed the other witnesses.

He swallowed and his head hurt and he felt his jaw muscles start to tremble, teeth chatter with grief. He breathed through his nose. There would be time for grief when this was done.

He looked back at Sam.

'The kid was found guilty,' he said. 'We hang him now. It ain't a choice.'

As he spoke, a knotted rope dropped down from the unfinished roof into the room.

He had known that something like this might happen. That despite everything they still might try and take it away from him. He'd planned for it. That was why he was who he was, why he was where he was. He had foresight. He planned for all eventualities.

'We don't even take him from this room,' Skunk McLean said, and raised his eyes to the sky.

As one everyone in the hall looked upwards. Where there had been cheering spectators previously, balanced up there on the walls, looking down through the unfinished roof, there were now a dozen of McLean's men, standing with rifles and revolvers pointed down into the room, silhouetted against the darkening sky.

'This is legal, this time,' McLean said. 'He's been found guilty and sentenced to hang. Now let's do it.'

Mort Mortensen stood on the plank-walk across the street from the hotel, corralled there with twenty or thirty other townsfolk by a group of cowboys he hadn't recognized. The cowboys had come out of the saloon earlier, maybe a dozen and a half of them and had joined the crowd outside the town hall, trying to gauge what was happening inside based on the cheers and laughter and yelling. They'd all known when the verdict was handed out, the sentencing, too. But then it had all got a little too hard to follow. All of a sudden there had been a lot of gunfire. Most of them outside on the street had figured it to be celebratory, but then one of the men up there on the roof had tumbled backwards and had crashed to the street. One of the women had started to rush towards the fallen man, but all of a sudden the cowboys from out of town had separated themselves from the spectators and had pulled guns and had marched the townsfolk back across the street. One of them had said, 'Verdict's in. We're just going to make sure no one stops us carrying out the sentence this time.' And Mortensen had seen other cowboys climbing up the walls, others with guns pointed at the men already up there, forcing them down, corralling them, too.

It was well planned and well executed. Men used to working together, men used to driving herds of beef or wagons trains of silver long distance maybe. Men used to controlling mine labourers. There were more gunshots from inside, more shouting, a little screaming.

Then silence.

And following the silence Mort saw one of the men on the roof throw a rope down into the room.

Ben Garcia looked upwards and counted nine men. One of them was holding the rope. The other eight had guns, all drawn and ready.

'Not in my court,' Judge Wilkes said, standing up. 'This is *not* happening in my court.'

McLean said, 'Sit down. Shut up.' His voice was stronger now. He was back in control.

'I will not—'

'Sit down! This is lawful. You've done your bit, Judge, and I thank you for that. We all thank you.'

'*You* will sit down. You will—'

A shot rang out from above and wood splinters exploded from the table in front of the judge.

Judge Wilkes glared at McLean.

'Sit down!' McLean said.

'This is contempt of court. *You* will be the next one on trial.'

'The court is over, Your Honour. You know that as well

as I do. Let us take care of business now.' He looked towards his two henchmen who had retaken their seats in the front row of the spectators' space. 'Boys.'

His men stood up.

'Put the rope around his neck.'

'Whoah, whoah!' Ben Garcia said, stepping forward. 'No, no, no.'

'No, no, no, yourself, Sheriff,' McLean said. 'You hand that boy over to my men now.'

Ben Garcia strode into the middle of the room. He turned and looked at the spectators. He looked at the crowd stood by the door. His townsfolk, the ones who paid him to keep things right in Hope. He held out his hands as if to say, *what can I do?* He looked at the judge, still standing there, jowly face red with anger, and then he let his eyes meet the eyes of the young man in the red vest. There was just a flicker of understanding. Then he looked back at Sam. The boy had been through too much, there was nothing left in the kid any more, emotion and life and belief were all gone. Garcia let his eyes slide across to Hector Lopez. Another moment of understanding.

'What can I do?' Ben Garcia said, looking back at McLean. 'All these people, they want to hang Sam a few days ago. I stop them then, no? You come again yesterday and I stop you again. But I can't stop it a third time, yes?'

'No. Yes. Whatever,' McLean said.

'I'm sorry,' Ben Garcia said to Sam, and walked over to the door, to the opposite side of the room from where he'd been positioned just a few seconds previously.

Ben Garcia watched Jim Cotton try to stand. Cotton's legs

were unsteady. He took a step forward and his left knee simply gave way. Jim looked up at McLean and shook his head.

'No, please.'

McLean spat in the dirt and turned away.

'Get the boy,' he said to one of his men. To the other he said, 'Get a chair.'

'You gonna let them do this?' someone said to Garcia from behind. He didn't turn to see who it was. 'It ain't right. Not like this.'

Sheriff Garcia said nothing. A silence had descended across the room. McLean's man pulled a chair into the centre of the room and McLean said 'No you fool, closer to the wall. You want the kid to swing like a pendulum and smash into the wall. He'd bring the whole place down.'

The other man grabbed Sam by the shoulder and marched him towards the wall, whilst the chair-man reached up and grabbed the noose. Garcia saw Jim Cotton reaching up with a hand, too exhausted and beaten to do anything more. He noticed how McLean avoided looking at the body of the girl who had been carried in.

Then, as the man with the noose said to Sam Cotton, 'Lower your head, kid,' and as everyone in the room was watching the boy, Ben Garcia nodded just once and drew his gun as fast as he could.

He shot three of the men standing on top of the wall on the side of the building that he could now see, the force of his bullets knocking the men backwards, their screams mixing with the report of his guns. Hector's shotgun roared twice, pointing to the roof above where Ben Garcia now stood. There must have been a wall behind the men on that side of the roof for one of the men fell inwards, screaming as he crashed down upon the spectators sat in the makeshift courtoom. They started yelling and hollering, too, some in surprise, and some in agony as bones were broken from the falling man. The judge's bodyguard took out three men from the far wall, his gun spitting fire and bullets so fast it sounded like a rattlesnake.

Within five seconds it was over. The only man standing on the roof was the one feeding the rope through his hands. He dropped the rope now and raised his hands high, a silhouette of defeat against the dark blue sky.

Skunk McLean's mouth dropped open. He raised his hands wide as if in disbelief.

'You killed them,' he said. 'They were doing nothing.'

The noise sounded, to Jim Cotton, like the initial volley of shots they had let loose against the rebels a lifetime ago in Glorieta Pass. The noise and the echoes and the screaming had gone on and on. Here, it was quicker, but in his beaten and exhausted mind he was no longer sure what was real and what wasn't.

He could hear shouting. Someone saying they were all killers and would pay for this. Then crying. Someone saying Amelia's name over and over. He thought it was his son, but that couldn't be right, he never had a son in the days of the war. It might have been his friend Skunk McLean. Skunk who never wanted to fight on account of all the money he had anyway.

The screams had given way to sobbing and now there was more gunfire, or was it banging, someone hammering, someone shouting 'Restrain that man! Restrain them all!'

Then 'We're taking a recess. We're not done here by a long way.'

Outside Mort Mortensen heard the roar of multiple gunshots and he saw the men on the roof get blown off the building and come crashing into the street below. A few of them lay silently, others moaned. The men standing guard over Mort and the others appeared confused not knowing what to do, and when Mort pushed his way passed them, running towards the courtroom, towards the greatest story of his life, none of them stopped him.

CHAPTER
FOURTEEN

Skunk McLean, and his two inside men, were bound and gagged.

Judge Wilkes said, 'I don't like to do it this way, but on account of you won't shut up this is the way it has to be.'

McLean twisted and turned against his bonds and his face looked so full of blood and anger that those still in the room feared he might explode.

It was fully dark now. The room was lit by numerous oil lamps. Scores of huge moths fluttered around and into the heads of all the people still crowded in there.

'Mr Cotton,' Judge Wilkes said, looking at Jim. 'Please tell us how you came by these gentlemen.' He pointed to Henry Herbert and to Dalton. Both were sat down on witness chairs against the side of the room from which McLean had wanted to hang Sam.

Jim Cotton stood up. They'd given him water, whiskey too.

After all the shooting, and after they'd wrestled Skunk

to the ground and tied him up, and after they taken the wounded spectators from the room – several of them under protest on account of no one wanted to miss a moment of the trial – he'd had chance to recover. He now held a tin cup of hot coffee laced with whiskey in his trembling hand.

'Skunk sent her away,' he said. 'Amelia, I mean.'

He saw McLean twisting and turning angrily on the chair he was tied to. Hector Lopez pressed down on the man's shoulders trying to keep him from tipping over.

The judge said, 'Skunk is?'

'That's Skunk. McLean.'

'And Amelia is?'

'His daughter. The girl I carried in.'

'The dead girl.'

'Yes.'

'Go on.'

'She was with Sam . . . when the shooting at the mercantile happened. But he' – Jim Cotton nodded at McLean – 'he had forbidden Amelia to see Sam. He said he would whip the skin off her legs if he found out she was seeing my boy.'

Whispers rose from the spectators. The judge picked up his hammer and the whispering ceased. Nobody doubted that Judge Wilkes meant what he said when he asked for silence any more. And nobody wanted to be ejected. This was just about the greatest trial since the days of Abe Lincoln.

'When Sam saw a bunch of riders chasing him down he thought it was McLean's men. That's why he rode away.'

The judge said, 'Hmm.'

'I went to see McLean the next day. The day after they tried to lynch Sam. I wanted to see Amelia, to ask her to tell the truth about where she and Sam had been the previous morning. She would have been able to prove my boy's innocence.'

McLean stared at Jim Cotton, fury in his eyes. His legs pressed on the floor, pushing up against Hector's hands.

'But he'd sent her away,' Jim Cotton said. 'That morning. Put her on the first stage East just so the truth couldn't come out.'

'And you went after her?'

'I did.'

'Then what?'

'The stagecoach had been attacked. The male passengers were killed.' Jim paused. 'They're still out there now, on the horses outside.'

'I saw.' The judge had taken the air a few moments earlier, whilst the sheriff, his deputy, and the judge's man had restored calm and order in the room – which in practical terms had meant restraining McLean and his two sidekicks.

When he'd come back in the judge had told both prosecutor and defender, Schwam and Rubin, that the trial was over, that *he'd* be asking the questions now in an effort to understand what was really going on here.

'But they'd taken the girl,' Jim Cotton said. 'Amelia.'

'Who's they?'

'The gang who'd attacked the stagecoach.'

'And you tracked them down?'

'I did.'

'One man?'

Jim Cotton sipped the coffee. His hands were no longer shaking. The events of the previous night didn't feel real. The only reality was this moment. When he'd first set eyes on the judge his heart had sank. Here was a man who looked more interested in food and whiskey and maybe a girl, and who no doubt wanted to dispense quick and popular justice to give himself as much time as possible to indulge in those interests. But looks were deceptive. The man had stood up to McLean. He'd not flinched at bullets and had even fired one of his own. And more than anything he was interested in the truth and ensuring justice was handled fairly – and Heaven help those that tried to sway it.

'Just me,' Jim Cotton said.

'How many were there in this gang?'

'I don't recall – six or seven.'

'And you . . . what? Killed them all?'

'All except him.'

Jim Cotton nodded at Dalton. The outlaw was also in handcuffs now.

'One man,' the judge said.

'Just me.'

'And you killed six or seven of them?'

'Yes, Your Honour. Well, Amelia killed one before they shot her.' When he said this both Sam and McLean's eyes widened. He couldn't read anything into either of their expressions. It might have been two men, she'd killed. He couldn't remember for sure. But the way Jim Cotton figured it, what had happened out there was just between him and God now. The precise details anyway.

'Hmm,' Judge Wilkes said.

'I had the element of surprise. They were drunk.'

'Unconscious drunk?'

'No, sir.'

The judge looked across at Dalton. 'Is that what happened?'

'I didn't see nothing and I didn't do nothing,' Dalton said. 'I never held up the store, and I never raped the girl. I was too drunk.'

At the mention of rape more whispers rose from the gallery and this time McLean jack-knifed so violently that the chair flipped on to its side. Hector Lopez and Henry Herbert righted the chair. Even with the two of them it was a struggle.

'But you did hold up the stagecoach?'

'I never killed no one.'

Judge Wilkes looked back at Jim Cotton. 'Who killed the girl?'

'One of the gang.'

'Go on.'

'I waited until they were asleep—'

'They were asleep?'

Jim Cotton stared at him.

'Sorry, go on.'

'I waited until they were asleep then I crawled in and cut the ropes they'd tied her with. We made it back out of their camp.'

'And?'

Jim Cotton looked across at McLean. 'If he'd never sent her away . . . he as good as killed her.' Both Hector Lopez and Henry Herbert were holding McLean down. Together they prevented him from flipping over the chair again.

Outside the courtroom several townsmen stood guard at the door with shotguns and rifles. They all suspected McLean had other men out there.

'What happened?' the judge said patiently.

'She'd been . . . she'd been through too much. The moment she was free she snatched a knife from my belt and ran back into the camp and stabbed one of them.'

'They killed her?'

'Yes. We would have got away . . . but that's when all hell broke loose.'

The judge looked at Dalton again. 'Is that how it was?'

Dalton nodded.

'I heard screaming and shooting. I was on guard down the trail. By the time I got into the camp it was all over. He'd killed them all and got the drop on me.'

'And is that it?' the judge said to Cotton. 'You then brought her home?'

'Yes. I mean, no, sir. There's more.'

'Go on.'

'He . . . the boy there, was alive. He told me he'd done it. He told me he was the one who had robbed the store and killed Jackson and Queenie and Ima, though he didn't know them of course.'

'So you killed him?'

'I brought him back. He died on the way.'

'Shame.'

'I can prove it,' Jim Cotton said.

'You can?'

'Yes, sir.'

Jim Cotton asked Henry Herbert to tell the judge what he

had already told Jim. Henry explained how the boy had ridden into the Junction on the day of the murders appearing nervous and scared. The coins were mentioned – coins that had come from Irwin Foote's mercantile. Jim Cotton explained how he had received some identical coins in his change from Irwin, and how, when he had passed one to the clerk at Black's Junction, that the clerk had mentioned he had seen some the same just a day before. Dalton, prompted by both Henry Herbert and Jim Cotton, said how the kid had boasted of doing the raid, of wanting to prove himself the equal of any other outlaw in their band.

Throughout the testimony McLean had twisted and turned and snorted against his bonds and his gag. His face had never been anything less than bright red.

'There are still some of the coins in the kid's pockets, I'd wager,' Jim Cotton said.

Judge Wilkes said, 'Hmm.'

'You Honour?' Jim Cotton said.

'It's a good story. I don't disbelieve you. But I wouldn't call any of it proof.'

'But—

The judge raised a hand.

'I'm not saying you did, but, *for example*, you could have put the coins in the young man's pockets yourself.'

McLean nodded violently.

Rube Rubin said, 'No more circumstantial than any of the evidence we heard earlier.'

The judge glared at Rubin then said, 'But I will agree that it does cast doubt on that evidence described earlier.'

Suddenly Tessa Brown leapt to her feet. 'Tell her what

you told me, 'she said, turning, looking at the seats next to her, then at the spectators, then back towards the judge. 'Where is she? Where's Martha?' she said.

'Excuse me,' Judge Wilkes said. 'Who are you? You gave evidence earlier, didn't you? For the boy, I believe.'

'I'm . . . Tessa Brown. Martha Kane . . . she just said . . . where is she?'

'What did Martha Kane just say, Tessa?' the judge asked, his voice patient but coloured with annoyance.

'She said . . . you know she had identified Samuel as the killer.'

'Yes, I know.'

'When she saw the . . . dead boy there . . . when she saw him she whispered to me that it could have been him. The dead boy, I mean. They all look alike, she said.'

Whispers rose from the spectators.

'Hush,' the judge said. 'Can someone go and find Martha Kane please?' he said, to no one in particular. Tessa Brown nodded. The judge added, 'Whilst we wait for Mrs Kane, is there anything else that you want to add?' He looked at Jim Cotton. 'Because if there isn't then I think it's only fair we allow Mr McLean to talk.'

Jim Cotton racked his brain. He'd done all he could, said all he could. It didn't feel like enough. The judge was looking at him as if it was all one big story. But what else was there? Jim knew *his* version of the story was the truth, but how could he make anyone else believe?

'Mr Cotton?' Judge Wilkes said 'Anything?'

'No, sir.'

'Then I propose we allow—'

'I'd like to say something, please,' the outlaw, Dalton,

said. 'It's a question you can ask of Mr McLean, sir.'

Jim Cotton looked across at Dalton. The man's tone of voice, his reverence to the judge, Jim wondered if the man was now thinking of his own immediate future.

The judge sighed. The increasingly cold air in front of his mouth clouded as he spoke. 'Go ahead.'

'Ask him why he hired us, sir.'

'Why he hired you?'

'Not me, sir, but all of us. It's not my gang. I'm no leader, sir. But we were hired by Mr McLean to rob a mule train heading from a silver mine in Hope out to the mills at Hell's Mouth. Might be an idea to ask him why would he want his own silver train robbed.'

The moment his gag was removed McLean started swearing and shouting, spittle flying from his mouth.

'Lies!' he shouted. 'It's all damn lies. They're making it up and you know it!' He glared at Judge Wilkes. 'You said so yourself: it's time to hang the boy. His father, too. He admitted he killed sleeping men out there. He was probably the one who raped and killed my daughter! He—'

The judge's hammer cracked down on the table.

'Silence! If you can't speak in a civilized—'

'It's all lies! I will not sit here gagged and unable to defend myself or my family. This is—'

'Silence!'

'That boy there could be anyone—'

'Silence! I won't tell you again.'

McLean gritted his teeth. The lower half of his face trembled with anger.

Judge Wilkes said, 'You are right – to a certain extent. I

can't say I'm seeing any proof. But . . . but that doesn't mean I'm prepared to listen to your ranting and raving, and it doesn't mean that the, uh, alternative version of events is not the truth. So, what do you say to this man's claim that you invited the gang of outlaws to rob your own silver train?'

McLean swallowed.

'I say it's nonsense. I say there's no proof. I say it's a crazy idea. Why on earth would I want anyone to steal my own silver?'

The judge stared at McLean. McLean stared back.

'Yes, I was wondering the same thing myself.'

'Because there is no silver,' Mort Mortensen said, standing up. He had managed to squeeze inside the room for the second half of this wonderful trial. 'The silver is all gone and he owes thousands of dollars to folks back East.'

McLean yelled that Mortensen was a liar, that the whole town were yellow-bellies, that they were scared to hang a man, but, by God, as soon as they untied him he would hang the boy, the father, and this lying pretend-journalist who said that his claim was all used up and the reason he wanted to rob his own non-existent silver train was to avoid having to pay investors back East.

The judge hammered on the table. The noise was high again as people yelled both for and against McLean, and now, increasingly, for Sam.

Another hammer crack.

'Don't you see what they're doing?' McLean cried. 'It's like the Indians using smoke to cover their retreat. That's what they do. They're just trying to hide the truth. We found the truth earlier!'

'Tell the goddamn truth yourself, McLean!' someone yelled.

'Let the boy go!' another replied.

'Hang McLean!'

'Hang 'em all – bound to get the guilty ones then!'

More laughter erupted.

The calm that had followed the recess was in danger of exploding again. Judge Wilkes had his man fire a warning shot once again, and then Wilkes said, 'I'm of a mind to lock you all up until morning. That'll give me time to sleep on things and try and figure out who's telling me the truth. I might want to take a look at your workings, too, Mr McLean, if that's OK.'

McLean glared at him.

'Is that OK, Mr McLean?'

'We've had some trouble out there, Your Honour. It's not safe at the moment. Indians, you understand?'

Judge Wilkes stared at him, and was about to speak and – several people said later they thought he was about to make an important statement – when the door opened and, for the final time in the trial, someone new made an entrance.

Martha Kane was positioned on one side of the stretcher; Tessa Brown the other. Two local men carried the stretcher, and on it lay Irwin Foote. He had been expected to die for several days but here he was, still breathing, now conscious again. Clearly in pain, very old and frail. The bandages around his lower face had been lowered revealing clotted blood and bruising and raw flesh. The shape of his mouth was wrong. But there was determination in his eyes.

Silence descended on the makeshift courtroom. Even Skunk McLean was quiet.

Martha Kane, now standing just inside the doorway, her face made yellow by a nearby oil lamp, said, 'When I saw the dead boy I suddenly realized that it *might* have been him, despite what I said earlier about—' She looked over at Sam Cotton. 'About Samuel. I still don't know. I . . . it's hard to tell when someone's dead. It happened with Jackson. The moment he was dead he was different. In looks, I mean.'

'When I went to find her,' Tessa Brown said, 'She was with Irwin. He was awake. Conscious for the first time since the shooting.'

'We thought it might be fate,' Martha said. 'Him waking just then.'

'Lift me up,' Irwin said, his lips hardly moving, his broken jaw not at all. 'Let me see.' The words were muffled.

'He, of all of us, will be able to tell who shot him,' Martha said.

'Lift me up,' Irwin said. 'Let . . . see . . . sonofabitch.'

The two men holding the stretcher laid it carefully on the floor then together they lifted Irwin up and helped him on to a chair. Irwin grimaced and several people noticed the sheen of tears in his eyes. The judge watched as Irwin looked at Sam and shook his head.

'Wasn't Sam,' he said. Then: 'Is that him under the blanket?' he asked, his voice surprisingly strong and clear all of a sudden.

'You tell us,' Ben Garcia said, and pulled the blanket back.

EPILOGUE

They stopped the wagon and the horses high on a ridge looking back down over the town of Hope.

It was an hour before dawn and in the half-light the town looked gentle and still. A silver tendril of smoke rose from Pigeon Parker's livery. Pigeon had been standing by the stable entrance when they'd left town. He'd nodded and lifted his coffee cup in a quiet salute. Jim Cotton had saluted military style in reply and Sam Cotton had smiled. No words had been necessary. The townsfolk of Hope had appeared to believe that words – all of those many sorrys and few we-never-really-thought-it-was-him – would be enough to make everything all right. But as Jim had told Sam time and again over the last few weeks, 'Words are cheap, son.'

The church clock – it didn't have any workings yet, but apparently the mechanisms were *en route* from Baltimore – reflected the colour of the lightening sky. A dog barked. Several hawks let the warming air lift them in gentle circles above the far side of town, their silhouettes disappearing and reappearing against the dark mountains beyond. Jim

Cotton could pick out the shape of the Domino saloon and the sheriff's office – he couldn't quite see the roof from where someone had once thrown down a knotted rope with which to hang his son – but he could picture it. No matter how hard he tried to forget he could always picture it. It felt like an age ago but it also gave him chills as if it had only happened that very morning. He could see the hotel and alongside it the hulk of the unfinished store-room in which the trial had been held. A little further along the main street he could see the edge of his old shop. The furnace was cold. The lawyer Rube Rubin had agreed to sell the premises – hopefully as a business – and forward the money to Jim Cotton. Once Jim Cotton had got to wherever he was going.

'Are you sad to be leaving?' Sam Cotton asked. He had a blanket wrapped around his shoulders. He was cold. Ever since the day they'd first tried to lynch him he'd been cold.

Jim Cotton looked across at his son. One thing he learned these last few weeks was what was important and what wasn't. And pretty much the only thing that was important was his family.

'Honestly?' he said.

'Honesty is the best policy,' Sam said. It was one of his mother's sayings.

'No,' Jim said. He watched the buzzards leave the town on the far side and head towards the wooded lower slopes of the foothills. 'There was a time when I thought I'd never leave, and if I'd been forced to then I'd have . . . I don't know. Wept, maybe. I fought for this place. I . . . I killed for this place.'

'I know.'

'But now . . . now I know that it's not the place that makes the place. It's the people that make it.'

'There's still some good folk down there.'

'I know.' Jim looked across at Sam. 'How about you?'

'You kidding?' Sam said. 'Crack that whip and get old Molly moving.'

Henry Herbert said, 'I heard you were leaving. I was hoping I'd heard wrong. It doesn't seem right. Or fair.'

They were in his lobby, in the shade. It was not yet noon but Henry had poured them all a beer from a new cask that had arrived just the day before.

'This is good beer, Henry,' Jim Cotton said.

Henry said, 'You're not wrong. I'm starting to try a little brewing myself. Slakes the thirst like whiskey never does, don't it?'

Samuel wiped his mouth with the back of his hand and said, 'I think you might be on to something here, Mr Herbert.'

'Call me Henry, son. I think we deserve to be on first names terms after what you've been through.'

'I wanted to thank you,' Sam said. 'For what you did. For everything.'

'You don't need to thank me.'

'We do,' Jim said. 'You did a lot more than you had to. You did more than anyone else did. A lot more.'

'Well, I'd like to say it was a pleasure. I mean, it was, helping you fellows. But at the time. All that shooting and fighting and . . . well, not knowing. Can't say it was a pleasure right then, if you know what I mean. Once it was over

. . . well, ever since I've been enjoying it. Never had an adventure like that in my life.'

'Me neither,' said Sam.

'I bet you don't want another.'

'That's a bet you'd win.'

They supped their drinks. Outside, through the open door, they could see the heat haze rising off the dirt and stones and they could see the blue sky, clear, and perfect.

'So where you boys headed?'

'North,' Jim said. 'We'd have headed straight up but it only seemed right to come and say goodbye.'

'I'm sorry to see you go.'

'Lot of folks are saying the same thing,' Jim said. 'But there weren't many like you who stood up for us when it mattered.'

'Hope is poison for us,' Sam said, finishing his beer, putting the glass down heavily. 'If I had a dollar for every one of them who says 'I knew you'd never really do something like that' then I'd be a rich man. But as far as I remember they were all in the crowd trying to hang me.'

'I hear they hanged no one in the end.'

Jim Cotton said, 'Dalton's still in the jailhouse waiting for some marshals from Albuquerque to come and get him. They wanted me to stick around to testify, but Ben Garcia understood. He said he wasn't going to keep me locked up just so I could tell everything one more time. I think he and Hec might be gone soon.'

'The town's poison,' Sam said again.

'And McLean?' Henry asked. 'I heard he's busted.'

Jim said, 'The seam ran dry a while ago. Or so the rumours go. He needed money to pay for wages and reinvestment to dig deeper. But no matter how much he poured into it the silver was all gone. I guess it had to run out sometime. The word is that he wasted too much on fancy living and on that big house and lake. They say he sold shares or took out a loan from some folks back East but couldn't pay anything back. And they say he figured setting up a robbery would buy him time. But those guys were wildcats. I saw them close up. They'd been robbing stagecoaches up and down the line for a while. Irwin's mercantile was just to pass the time whilst McLean got his mule train of stone together. They say McLean's still terrified that the truth will get out. He was furious with them for bringing attention to the town but by getting Sam here lined up for the crime he figured no one would dig long enough or hard enough to uncover the truth. But that journalist fellow – the Scandinavian – did just that. If they'd have lynched Sam that first night none of this would have come out.'

'Is it all true?'

'Damn right,' Sam said.

'But they couldn't prove it?'

'No. That's his point. He says we just made a big smoke-screen of confusion.'

Herbert nodded.

'Fate's a strange thing,' he said. 'It usually gets you in the end.'

Jim Cotton said, 'I don't care about McLean anymore. We were friends once upon a time. But what do kids know? Last I heard he's still mad as hell and is vowing to hang us all. Says he believes I killed Amelia and maintains Sam was the mercantile robber. Like I said he contends everything else was just a ruse to get Sam off.'

'I think he's a little bit crazy,' Sam said, picking up his beer glass, looking at the emptiness within. 'And he wanted Ben to arrest Father for killing all those outlaws. They should have made him a hero.'

'*That* I agree with.'

'McLean keeps on about how those men were drunk and asleep and that Father is nothing but a coward.'

'It doesn't matter,' Jim said.

Sam put his empty glass down.

'Would you like another,' Henry asked. 'On the house, of course. It's mighty dusty and dry out there'

Sam looked at Jim. 'Father?'

Suddenly someone started yelling. They heard and felt the pounding of a horse's hoofs on the hard ground, heard someone calling for a horse to *whoah.*

Outside, a barefoot man in blue dungarees and a dirty white undershirt was holding the reins of a horse that was foaming at the mouth and slick with sweat.

On the horse was a woman, her face caked with dust, her hair wild from the wind, her eyes full of fear.

Jim Cotton took a moment to recognize her, but when he did his mouth fell open in shock. 'Laurie,' he said. 'Laurie McLean. My God, what happened?'

Her eyes locked on to his and when recognition came to her she reached out her hands and almost fell off the horse into his arms.

She was still shaking an hour later, but a jug of water, two whiskies, and a glass of the beer that had recently arrived from the east had calmed her enough that she could talk.

153

'They're all dead,' she said.

'All?' asked Jim?

'Who?' Henry Herbert said.

'All of them. Those who hadn't already gone. Those who weren't killed that night in town.'

She looked up at Jim, at Henry, at Sam, and they all saw the tears and the darkness in her eyes combining to make dark pools of pain. Most everyone from Black's Junction had crowded into the lobby of the hotel to hear Laurie's story and Herbert had had to regularly admonish everyone to give her space, to let her breathe. But they were all still there, around the edges of the room, no one wanting to miss a moment. It reminded Jim of the makeshift courtroom back in Hope, everyone intent on hearing every word of someone else's misfortune. Just after Laurie had arrived they'd found an arrow caught in the gap between her saddle and the horse's flesh. The fact that the Indians were involved made everyone even more interested. That and who she was (over the last few weeks Henry Herbert had told, retold, and exaggerated his tale of what McLean had done and what had happened in the courtroom) meant even more interest from the Junction's inhabitants.

Tears escaped from Laurie's eyes and created dark brown tracks through the white dust on her face. 'I knew the moment he sent Amelia away that everything was going to go wrong.' She looked up at Jim. 'When I heard she was dead I knew that it hadn't all gone wrong, it had all gone to hell.'

Jim Cotton reached out and rested his hand on her wrist.

'It's OK, Laurie.'

He of all people knew what it was like to lose almost everything.

'He's dead,' she said.

'Skunk?'

She nodded. Whispers ran round the room like fire jumping from one dry bush to the next.

'What happened?' Henry said quietly.

'It was all true,' she said. 'The rumours, I mean. The silver was all worked out – he never told me. I had no idea, but a few days ago he was drunk.' She looked up at Jim. 'He was often drunk. More so recently.' She lifted the beer glass, then realized what she'd just said and put it down again.

'It's OK,' Jim said. 'One drink doesn't make you a drunk.'

She managed a thin smile and took a sip.

'He told me . . . when he was drunk, I mean. He told me it was all true. We had no money. We were ruined. He'd borrowed money from some investors back East to work the mine further and deeper.' Now she looked at Henry. 'He was a good man, really. I know . . . I know what happened . . . but he was trying to find a way to keep it all going for all of us, not just me and . . . Amelia . . . all the men, the town. He dug deeper but there was nothing. Other claims had sprung up. There was nothing, so he tried . . . he tried to make some money by running cattle and other things, but silver was all he knew. He lost more money than he made on anything other than silver.' She shook her head and more tears rolled down her face.

'It's all right,' Henry said, 'Take your time.'

'And then they hated us in town. That night . . . so

155

many men died. So many of our men. It was terrible. He changed. He wanted to kill you all. He wanted to burn the whole town down. He'd drink and he'd get his guns out and. . . .' She looked at Sam. 'Sometimes he'd cry. He felt so much guilt.'

'It's OK,' Sam said quietly.

'But the men left,' she said. 'One by one. There was just a half dozen there this morning when. . . .'

She lifted the drink again, her hand was shuddering and the beer spilled on to Henry's polished table.

'He used to pay them off. The Apache, I mean. Horses. Guns. Whiskey. But he didn't even have money left for that.'

'So they came?' Henry said.

She nodded. 'The men . . . the few who were still there fought and fought but . . . They burned everything. Everything they couldn't carry. Everything,' she said. 'There's nothing left.'

Now the tears came in rivers.

Later, when she was able to talk again, she recounted how one of the men, the one called Mitchell, had taken her to the stables and saddled the fastest horse they had. 'Run for town,' he'd told her. 'Head for Hope.' But the Hope trail had been blocked by Apaches – she'd seen them in the distance – and she had instead cut across towards Black's Junction, pushing the horse as hard as she could, never daring to look behind.

'Once or twice I could hear them so close,' she said, her hands trembling again. 'They were near enough for arrows, but then . . . I think when I started to get near here they either backed off or maybe they tired. I don't know.'

She looked up, and this time she stared at all of them in turn. But there were no more words.

Henry Herbert put them all up in the hotel overnight. He cooked them a fine dinner and availed them of the bathroom. Over coffee and bacon the next morning, with Sam still asleep in his room, Laurie McLean said to Jim Cotton, 'You're leaving, then?'

'Yes.'

'It was our fault?'

'No. Not you. Not even Skunk, really. Skunk was the . . . I don't know, he was the oxygen that made the fire hotter. But the way those folks turned on Sam. On us. Our life in Hope . . . I think we'd lived it out. It's time. It's that simple.'

'Where will you go?'

He shrugged.

She sipped coffee from an elegant china cup.

For a long time neither spoke. He watched her drink. He studied her whilst she was looking down at her plate, running her fingertips over the clean linen table cloth, whilst she gazed out of the window at the morning. He recalled feelings from many years ago. But too much sand had blown along the trail. They were very different people now. They'd both made decisions about life, about partners, about everything. She'd chosen someone other than him. She was a mother, he was a father. She a widow, he a widower. Both still grieved. He'd become a killer and knew he was changed forever by what had happened all those years ago and again just those few weeks ago. His patience wasn't what it once was. His faith now wavered. But his love was stronger. And he now felt those feelings – maybe memories – again. He thought of Tessa Brown and how much she had wanted a romance with him. But there had never been anything there, not for him. And she – Tessa – was too much of the town, too much part of what he needed to be away from. Anyway, he had loved – and still loved – Mary more than any other woman. He looked at Laurie again. There had been a time, long ago, when he'd felt the same about her. Had fate chosen otherwise then both their lives might have been very different. Maybe all it had taken was to be a little late on the Hope-Hell's Mouth run that one time. It was the same with Sam; had he chosen another morning to have met Amelia then they'd all have been riding along a very different trail.

He realized she was looking back at him.

'What are you thinking, Jim Cotton?' she said.

She was still beautiful – or would be again once the pain and fear and memories had their edges dulled – but it wasn't that. It was their history and a future that once might have been. He felt guilt rising up, but it didn't put up much of a fight when he pushed it down. He was doing nothing wrong. He wasn't making any promises; he wasn't guessing which way the cards would fall. All he was doing was letting the horses and the stagecoach find their own way over the worst of the ruts whilst ensuring he controlled it from getting totally out of hand.

'Jim?' she said.

'You should come with Sam and me,' he said. 'I don't know where we're going and I don't know what we're going to find when we get there. I'm not making any promises and I'm certainly not—'

She put her hand on his.

'Jim.'

'I just think, maybe . . . we could even go our separate ways when we get to wherever—'

'Jim.'

'I mean, we don't have to. We need to . . . it'll be like that time when Skunk and I headed West all those years ago. Neither of us knew what life would bring. It was a good feeling. It's a new start, Laurie, it's—'

'Jim.'

He looked at her.

'You're crying,' he said. 'I didn't mean . . . is it a bad idea?'

'It's a very good idea,' she said. 'Thank you.'

Later that morning, they set off for the north, talking of farms and fertile land, of peace and safety, even of brewing beer. They had a good mule and a fine horse and a wagon-load of provisions. They found they could speak freely of the events of the last few weeks, the last few years, the last many years. Sam, at first a little reticent and quiet, soon came to see that all they were was a group of pioneers heading across the plain to a new future.

That afternoon a huge flock of geese crossed their path, migrating to their own new life. At one point, when a wind, colder than expected, blew across from the north-east, Laurie shuddered and instinctively reached out and gripped Jim's hand. He squeezed her hand and didn't let go.

It hurt, all the memories, the loss, the pain and the dying and the killing. But it was good, too, that hurt. It allowed one to move on whilst holding on to all that had gone before.

He looked across at Laurie and then to Sam.
'Is it OK?' he asked.
'It will be,' Laurie said. 'It will be.'
Sam nodded. 'It's going to be fine,' he said.
And they drove northwards.